THE GHOST COLLECTOR

THE GHOST COLLECTOR

ALLISON MILLS

annick press
toronto • berkeley

Copyedited by Mary Ann Blair
Proofread by Rhonda Kronyk
Cold read by DoEun Kwon

Cover illustrated by Natasha Donovan
Designed by Paul Covello

We acknowledge the support of the Canada Council for the Arts and the Ontario Arts Council, and the participation of the Government of Canada/la participation du gouvernement du Canada for our publishing activities.

Library and Archives Canada Cataloguing in Publication
Title: The ghost collector / Allison Mills.
Names: Mills, Allison, author.
Identifiers: Canadiana (print) 20190070471 | Canadiana (ebook) 2019007051X | ISBN 9781773212951 (softcover) | ISBN 9781773212968 (hardcover) | ISBN 9781773212999 (PDF) | ISBN 9781773212975 (Kindle) | ISBN 9781773212982 (EPUB)
Classification: LCC PS8626.I45 G56 2019 | DDC jC813/.6—dc23

Published in the U.S.A. by Annick Press (U.S.) Ltd.

Distributed in Canada by University of Toronto Press.

Distributed in the U.S.A. by Publishers Group West.

Printed in Canada

allisonmillswrites.com
annickpress.com

Also available as an e-book. Please visit annickpress.com/ebooks for more details.

MIX
Paper from
responsible sources
FSC® C004071

For Louisa and Lois

BEFORE

1

Shelly's grandma teaches her about ghosts, how to carry them in her hair. If you carry your ghosts in your hair, you can cut them off when you don't need them anymore. Otherwise, ghosts cling to your skin, dig their fingers in under your ribs, and stay with you long, long after you want them gone.

Shelly's mother doesn't like ghosts. She doesn't like Grandma telling Shelly about them. It's an old argument, one they have every time Grandma gives Shelly a lesson. "You'll scare her," she says, like Shelly isn't in the room. "You'll keep her up at night."

"How is she going to take care of herself if she can't take care of the dead?" Grandma asks, and Shelly's mother never has much of an answer for that. So Grandma teaches Shelly about ghosts, how to keep them, and how to get rid of them— not just her own ghosts but other people's, too. Shelly likes to think of herself as her grandma's apprentice.

Today, Grandma's client is a woman clad in expensive

yoga pants with her hair in a high ponytail. "We burned sage," the woman says. She tours Shelly and Grandma around her haunted apartment—it's bright and airy, much bigger than the old duplex Shelly and her mom and grandma share. "To cleanse it, you know?"

Grandma smiles, all bland and pointed, and Shelly stifles a laugh with her hand at the image of this yoga lady waving her spice rack around, trying to exorcise her apartment. "To cleanse it?"

"From the . . . spirits. The demons. You know." The woman gestures vaguely at Grandma, at her soft brown skin and warm brown eyes, at the little turtle earrings she wears every day. The things that make some people say *Native*, but Grandma corrects them and says *Ililiw* or *Cree*. "It's cleansing. The smoke. We fanned it around the whole house and nothing. The spirits are still here."

Shelly can see the ghost that haunts the lady's apartment dancing around her feet. It's a little dog with a constantly wagging tail, trotting around on tiny paws with nails that clack against the hardwood floors and echo through the hallways. It noses its way over to Shelly and Grandma like it wants to play.

Grandma keeps smiling, her eyes on the woman and not the ghost dog. "I don't use sage to cleanse ghosts."

"Oh. So it's like . . . for other stuff? Bad juju?"

Grandma turns her back on the woman. "This is a tough case," she says and winks at Shelly. "I might have to charge a *little* more for the work. Do you mind?"

Grandma heads deeper into the apartment, listening to the woman talk seriously about the sound of claws scraping over the floors and the cold wind that blows around her ankles whenever she comes home—about how she feels like the spirits want her gone, and isn't it weird that her brand-new condo is haunted like this?

Shelly takes a seat in the hallway and clucks her tongue at the dog, smiling. She's never had a pet before—too expensive—but she likes dogs. A ghost dog would be a good pet—ghosts don't need feeding the same way living beings do.

"It's okay," she tells the dog, leaning toward it so Grandma's client won't hear her whispering. She tugs the tie off the end of the braid Grandma wove her long, dark hair into and combs her fingers through it, loosening it. "Grandma and I are going to take you for a walk."

The dog's tail wags even harder and Shelly lets it dance

around her, nipping at the ends of her hair as she waits for Grandma to finish talking to the woman about the monster she imagines is hiding under her bed.

People are always coming by the house to see if Grandma will get rid of their ghosts—cats that wind around their ankles and trip them when they walk. Dogs that bark in the middle of the night, startling them out of sleep.

Shelly catches the dog in the ends of her hair then scoops it into her arms when Grandma and the woman come back into the hallway, scratching it under the chin. Holding it is like holding a cold wind, and when the puppy licks her face it feels like someone is rubbing an icicle against her cheek.

"Will this take long?" the lady asks, getting her wallet out of her purse. "Is $300 enough?"

Three hundred is a lot for a ghost. Most of Grandma's clients pay in knickknacks and favors and food. Grandma doesn't normally charge much because if people know they have a ghost, they might pay anything to get rid of them—do anything.

"Not long at all," Grandma promises. "We'll be out of here before you know it."

They walk the dog to the park, and Shelly and the dog play

fetch with an invisible stick until the dog fades away, finally ready to rest.

They go home and Shelly helps Grandma out of her coat. Shelly's mother is in the kitchen and there's a frozen lasagna in the oven.

"You've got to be responsible," Grandma tells Shelly. "You can't charge people through the nose to get rid of a ghost."

Mom looks over from putting her hair up to go to work, her uniform shirt all nicely pressed. Her hair is long, like Grandma's and Shelly's, but she almost never wears it down outside the house. She doesn't want anything clinging to it.

"I made dinner for you and Shelly." Mom points a finger at Grandma as the oven timer goes off. "You could charge a little more."

"We've got to undercut the frauds so people come to us instead. We can help people," Grandma says, pulling the lasagna out of the oven. "Sit and eat before you go."

"Someone has to pay the bills," Mom says, but she sits and cuts up the lasagna in its tinfoil pan. "What about helping *us*?"

The duplex they rent isn't anything like the fancy apartment Shelly and Grandma spent the afternoon in. The floors creak when it's cold and the front door opens right into the kitchen because there's no space wasted. The cabinets are sturdy wood but old, and every room has orange wallpaper Shelly's mother hates but can't change because they're renting. She did cover Shelly's walls with posters of cats and dogs and other pets Shelly likes but can't have to help make the room look nicer, though.

Shelly's bedroom is the smallest one. With her dresser shoved into the doorless closet, there's enough room for her bed and a bookshelf but not much else, especially since she tends to leave her clothes on the floor—clean things folded and stacked neatly, dirty clothes in a heap in the corner—instead of putting them away where they belong. The only thing Shelly puts away is a sweater, blue with an orange cat on the front. Shelly and her mom found it brand-new at the thrift store and it always goes in a drawer because it's Shelly's favorite. The room feels softer and more lived in around the edges with clothes everywhere—more comfortable.

Grandma grabs her purse as she sits at the table, pulling out the money she and Shelly made for the ghost dog. "Is this useful?"

Mom looks surprised. "For just one ghost?"

"The lady was rude," Shelly says, leaning over to scoop noodles from the pan and onto her plate. "She talked about burning sage to cleanse the spirits from her home, but it was just a little dog."

Mom laughs, setting the cash down on the table. "*One of those clients*," she says. "You need to get more rich people who don't know anything about the dead—this is the kind of money we need around here."

"It was a one-time thing," Grandma says, shaking her head. "I don't want to seem like some kind of fraud."

"You go around telling people you can clear out *ghosts*. You already seem like a fraud." Mom serves Grandma some lasagna then serves herself. "If you don't want rude women with small dogs making assumptions about you, maybe don't offer to be the brown woman they bring in to spiritually clean their house."

Grandma frowns at Mom. "We're not a stereotype."

"Mom, you're a bit of a stereotype."

"It was a cute dog," Shelly says loudly. "A ghost dog would make a good pet, don't you think? You wouldn't have to buy food or take it to the vet."

Mom and Grandma both turn to look at her.

"You can't keep ghosts hanging around like that," Grandma says. "Everyone has to move on eventually—maybe in their own time, but it's not fair to hold someone captive."

"She knows, Mom," Shelly's mother said, plainly amused. "While I support a pet that costs no money, you're around death more than enough as it is, Shell. Nobody in this house needs haunting. The dead are dead, and that's the way it should be. Leave them alone."

"They're dead, but sometimes they need help passing over," Grandma says. "Then we've got a *responsibility* to help them move on."

That's how it is most of the time. Mom worries about money and whether Shelly will get nightmares. Grandma keeps calm and steady—more sure of herself than anyone else Shelly knows.

Shelly is the only person in the sixth grade who knows, deep in her bones, that ghosts exist. She knows that because Ms. Flores assigns the class a presentation about what they want to be when they grow up—a teacher or an actor or a chef—and drops them off at the school library with Mrs. Hogan, the librarian, to do research.

"My dad's a professor, so I'm going to write about being a physicist," Isabel says, while she and Shelly are searching the non-fiction section for books. Isabel and Shelly aren't *friends*, exactly, but their desks are beside each other and Shelly likes Isabel. She's Korean and wears her long, dark hair loose like she's not afraid of what might get caught in it. Isabel dresses in bright colors and always has new clothes. She's nice though—some of the other kids single Shelly out for being brown, for being the only Indigenous kid in their class. Isabel doesn't. Isabel tells them to knock it off. "I don't really *need* a research book to write about it."

"My grandma is a ghost hunter," Shelly says. "I'm going to be one, too."

Isabel gives Shelly a skeptical look. "Ghosts don't exist. My dad's a scientist. I think he'd know if ghosts were real. Someone *serious* would be studying them."

"They do. I've seen them. Grandma takes me with her on jobs sometimes." Shelly knows people don't always believe they're being haunted, but it's the truth. Ghosts are as real as she and Isabel are.

"They don't," says a voice behind her, and Shelly turns to see Lucas, the tallest kid in fifth grade, with a book on forensics tucked under his arm. "Ghosts are made up."

Shelly's used to people not believing in ghosts, but it's still frustrating to have people argue with her when she *knows* they're real. She shakes her head. "I've talked to plenty of ghosts before."

"You haven't because they're not real." Lucas holds up the book in his hands. "Show me proof of ghosts if you want me to believe you."

"Did everyone find what they were looking for?" Mrs. Hogan asks, looming out of the stacks. She looks at them like she knows they were arguing.

"Yes," says Lucas.

"I have a book," says Isabel.

Shelly wishes she'd picked something up right away, but she's not sure the library has anything she could use. "I haven't found one yet."

Mrs. Hogan turns her attention to Shelly. "Shelly, can I talk to you for a moment? You've still got lots of time to find your book."

Shelly knows where this is going. Mrs. Hogan doesn't believe in ghosts either. "Yes, Mrs. Hogan."

Shelly follows her across the library to the small circulation desk. Mrs. Hogan turns to her, expression disapproving. "I know you mean well, and your grandma works as a . . . psychic, Shelly, but you really shouldn't go around telling your classmates ghost stories," she says. "You might give them nightmares."

Adults will sometimes believe Grandma when she talks about ghosts and hauntings, but they never believe Shelly. They're like her mom—always more worried about bad dreams than the dead. Not everyone can see ghosts, even when they see the evidence of their presence. People look at Shelly and think she must be making up stories, especially adults. Especially *teachers*.

When Grandma talks about ghosts, people are more likely to listen. They don't roll their eyes at her or tell her she's making up stories to give people bad dreams. Grandma's got age on her side. Even if people decide they don't believe her after all, they let her finish speaking.

Most people think the dead are just gone, that they vanish with no transition period. Most people don't ever get a chance to see ghosts the way Shelly and her grandma and mom can—even if her mom just works at the drugstore instead of busting ghosts with Grandma.

It's a gift that runs in the family, like their dark hair and long noses and big brown eyes—women can see ghosts. Grandma's mother could see ghosts, and her mother's mother could, too. Grandma tells stories sometimes about when she lived up north, before she got married and moved down to the city with her white husband, who became her ex-husband. People would knock on her mother's door and ask for help making sure their loved ones had moved on. Everyone knew she had a knack for speaking with the dead, even if they didn't know exactly how she did it. Shelly wants that, too. Growing up in the city instead of up north, Shelly feels like she only gets bits and pieces of what it means to be Cree.

Her mom talks politics, but that's only one part of it, and other than her family the only Indigenous people Shelly knows are their neighbors. Ghost hunting is a way to connect with the people who came before her. It's got history, the same way ghosts do.

Grandma's mother never charged anything for her services, but times have changed and Grandma and Mom need to pay rent.

"I wasn't saying anything scary." Shelly does her best not to frown at Mrs. Hogan. "I was just talking about ghosts. Isabel's dad is a professor so she's writing about being a professor. My grandma hunts ghosts, so I'm going to write about being a ghost hunter."

Mrs. Hogan doesn't look like she believes Shelly, but she doesn't say no to her idea either. "We have a few books on parapsychology," she says. "And some on spiritualism and debunking urban legends. They might be a good place for you to start your research. Do you want me to help you find them in the catalog?"

Shelly lets Mrs. Hogan show her where to find the books. It's easier than arguing. People at school are weird about ghosts. They don't take her seriously. It's obvious that Mrs.

Hogan thinks ghost hunting is like one of the TV shows Grandma scoffs at, where a bunch of people run around old hospitals with infrared cameras in the dark and scare themselves. That's not how Grandma works. She finds ghosts that need help and she helps them. No special equipment required.

Shelly sits down at her assigned table at the end of the library while they wait for Ms. Flores to come walk them back down the hall, and Lucas gives her books a judgmental look. "That's all made up," he says.

"The library doesn't have any books on real ghosts," Shelly says. "It's passed down in my family."

"So it's made up." Lucas is smug. "I knew it."

Shelly frowns at him. "It's not made up just because you don't know about it and nobody wrote about it in a book. You don't know everything."

"Lucas. Shelly." Mrs. Hogan stops beside their table. "Do I need to tell Ms. Flores you were arguing in class?"

Lucas sits up straighter in his chair. "No, Mrs. Hogan."

Shelly wants to say Lucas started it, but Mrs. Hogan already pulled her aside once today. "Sorry," she says. "We'll stop."

Shelly knows she's right and that will have to be enough.

• • •

Shelly's mother picks her up from school in her old, beat-up car. Its windshield is cracked and the radio always sounds staticky because the antenna is broken. The rearview mirror is held in place with glue and hope. Her mom's hair is up in a messy ponytail and she's dressed for work, shirt rumpled after her shift. She looks tired. "How was school?" she asks, smiling. "Learn anything exciting?"

"We're doing a project on what we want to be when we grow up," Shelly says, climbing into the car and dropping her red backpack on the floor. It's about as shabby as the car because she got it secondhand. Most of her clothes come from the thrift store, another thing that makes Shelly different from other kids. "Nobody believes in ghosts."

"Oh no, Shelly—you told your teachers you wanted to be like Grandma?" Her mom looks both exasperated and amused. "Shell, you *know* people don't like thinking about ghosts. *I* don't like thinking about ghosts and I grew up with your grandma."

"Why not?" Shelly asks. "There's nothing wrong with ghosts."

"They're dead," her mom says. "They're dead and we're alive. Those are two very different things. To everyone else it sounds like superstition."

"Mrs. Hogan said I shouldn't talk about ghosts in class or I'd scare the other kids." Shelly doesn't think that's true. Isabel and Lucas didn't believe her, but they weren't *afraid*. Besides, what Shelly's learning from her Grandma is more important than making friends at school. The dead don't care how new your shoes are or what kind of job your parents have.

"Mrs. Hogan isn't wrong. I had bad dreams about ghosts all the time when I was a kid." Her mom turns the car on and pulls away from the curb. "I *knew* they were real. I think not knowing for certain would be even scarier."

"Why were you scared?" Shelly asks because it baffles her—ghosts are just a part of life. "Ghosts are just people."

Her mom is quiet for a moment, either thinking or concentrating on the road. "Ghosts *aren't* just people," she says. "I mean, they are, but they're more than that—they're people *plus*. They've been through everything you and I are ever going to go through, you know? They went through their whole lives and something kept them here even though they

16

should've moved on to whatever comes next. Your grandma gets rid of ghosts because they're out of step with the rest of the world." She glances at Shelly. "I wouldn't wish that on my worst enemy.

"People are afraid of ghosts because they know more than we do. They know what it feels like to live their whole lives and now they're hanging in between here and the other side—not in one place or the other." She shrugs. "I can't blame people for not wanting to think about being trapped like that."

"If someone can see you and talk to you, are you trapped?" Shelly asks. "We can see ghosts."

"Sure," says her mom, "but sometimes you might want to talk to someone else and you couldn't. I mean, I'd never get tired of talking to you, Shell, but you might get tired of talking to me, don't you think?"

Shelly looks at her mother and grins. "Yeah, I would," she agrees. "I'd get bored. You'd *have* to let me have a pet then."

Her mom laughs, and that's the end of the ghost talk, but Shelly can't help thinking that she's wrong. Ghosts aren't scary at all.

3

When they pull into their gravel driveway, Mrs. Potts is waiting by her front door. She lives in the other half of their duplex with just her two cats. Shelly's pretty sure she and Grandma are about the same age, but Mrs. Potts wears a lot of cardigans with seasonal embellishments and keeps her gray hair short and in curls. It makes her seem older.

That and the cats.

"Hi!" Mrs. Potts says, as they get out of the car. Her cardigan today is black with orange and yellow felt leaves stitched to its front. Even looking at it makes Shelly feel itchy. "Amanda, I was just heading over to say hello to your mom."

"I'm sure she'll be happy for the visit, Edna," Shelly's mom says, with a look on her face that says, *Oh no, we're trapped.* Mrs. Potts is very good at talking. Her daughter is a police officer and visits at least once a week—Mrs. Potts likes to brag about her. "I could go grab her."

"Oh, no trouble," says Mrs. Potts. "I'm on my way out the

door, but I wanted to invite you for dinner tonight. Jenny's coming over and I'm going to roast a chicken. There'll be more than enough food for the two of us. I thought it might be nice."

"Oh," says Shelly's mom, who doesn't really like cats or Mrs. Potts very much. "I don't know, we wouldn't want to intrude . . ."

Mrs. Potts shakes her head. "Nonsense. I'd love the company."

Shelly's mother looks annoyed, but not enough to say no. "Thank you, Edna," she says. "Can we bring anything? Dessert?"

"Dessert would be lovely," Mrs. Potts says, smiling. "Come over around five."

Shelly's mom waits for Mrs. Potts to go back inside then looks down at Shelly. "Okay, well, I'm going to go buy a pie at the grocery store," she says. "Tell Grandma we got ambushed and I'll be home in half an hour."

"Sorry, Mom," Shelly says, grinning up at her. Going to Mrs. Potts's house isn't too bad—she gets to play with the cats. "Apple?"

"Apple," Mom agrees.

• • •

Jenny Potts answers the door when they knock. Her short hair is a brown so dark it almost looks black, and she's dressed in jeans and a T-shirt, not like a cop at all. Shelly's not used to seeing her in anything but her uniform. "I'm sorry about this," she says, stepping aside so they can enter. "Mom's got a bee in her bonnet."

"I don't have a bee in my bonnet, I have ghosts in my house!"

Shelly's mother, carrying a pie from the *nice* grocery store, the one that bakes things from scratch, looks immediately and thoroughly unimpressed. "Ghosts."

"I told her she should just talk to your mom if she's worried she's being haunted, but . . ." Jenny shrugs. "She wanted to have you over for dinner."

Grandma laughs and pushes past Jenny into the house. "Edna, let's see what we can do," she says. "It might just be the cats."

"I can tell the difference between a cat and a ghost," Mrs. Potts says. "I might not talk to spirits, but I know my cats."

"Can I help?" Shelly asks, looking up at her mom. Normally

she'd just do it, but with her mother there, asking seems important.

Mom hesitates but nods. "You can help." She looks at Jenny. "It'll be something small, if it's anything."

"Drinks?" Jenny suggests. "While they do ghost things?"

"Please," says Shelly's mom.

Mrs. Potts's duplex is a mirror of their own. Shelly follows Grandma and Mrs. Potts through the kitchen and down the hallway. Mrs. Potts uses the big room—the one Shelly's mom uses for a bedroom—as a living room. The cats are curled up together on the couch, and Shelly can hear the ghosts under the floor as soon as she steps inside the room.

"Oh," she says. "It's *mice*."

"Mice?" Mrs. Potts repeats, alarmed. "Louisa, I promise you I don't have mice. The cats hunt anything that tries to get in."

"No, Edna, *ghost* mice," says Grandma. "Your cats are probably the reason you're having an issue. They're doing too good a job."

Mrs. Potts relaxes a bit, walking over to give one of the cats a pat. "They do like to bring me back presents."

Shelly can see why her mom isn't a big fan of cats. Ghosts

are one thing—dead mice are another. "It sounds like they're in the floor," Shelly says, sitting down on the rug and knocking on it. A skittering sound under the floorboards makes Mrs. Potts shiver. Mice *shouldn't* be hard to get rid of, but Shelly's never had to get ghosts out of a floor before.

Grandma reaches up to undo her braided hair and lets it fall out, loose and free. "What do you think about the air vents?" she asks Shelly. "I think they could work."

Animal ghosts tend to be simple—the spirits of creatures that haven't realized they're dead yet. Being outside helps them fade away because a ghost removed from an anchor— whether that's its home, where it died, a favorite place, or a grave—will start to fade unless someone tries to keep it around. The dead aren't made to stick around in the world of the living forever, although some ghosts are stronger than others, more concrete and settled in their death.

Shelly and her grandma use their hair like a net, like a fishing lure. They let ghosts cling to them and act as a hook to carry the dead to new places, places where they won't be tied to anything and will be able to fade. Sometimes they offer comfort—they burn sweetgrass and feed ghosts warm milk—and sometimes they just let a spirit fade, let it travel to where it's going because it doesn't need much more than a nudge to carry on.

Shelly doesn't really want to stick her hair down an air vent and hope it gets full of mice, but the vents are in the floor and Grandma is old.

"Vents might work," she says. "I can do it."

"Your mother is going to kill me," says Grandma. "Then she's going to regret killing me when I come back to haunt her."

Shelly laughs and undoes her ponytail, scooting across the rug to the nearest vent. She carefully lowers her hair down through the grate and then looks up at Grandma and Mrs. Potts. "Do I just sit and wait?" she asks. "How many mice do you think—"

"Shelly!" Shelly turns her head, looking at her mom standing in the doorway of the room with Jenny. "What are you doing? Mom, *what?*"

"It's mice," says Shelly, trying not to frown. She knows what she's doing. She's carried around bigger ghosts than *mice* before. "I'm just getting them out."

"Your hair is going to be full of ghosts *and* cat hair. Shell, pull back please. There's got to be another way."

"I was going to do it myself," Grandma says. "Shelly wanted to try."

"You shouldn't be sticking your hair down vents either, Mom," Shelly's mother says. "This is a bad plan."

Shelly feels a tug on the ends of her hair—one tug, followed by a bunch more all at once. She lifts her head up carefully and the ghosts come out with her, passing easily through the grate. Ghosts are spirits and spirits don't care about things like barriers unless they *want* to care about them. Ghosts can touch people and things, but people and things can't touch ghosts—not unless they're like Shelly and her family.

Shelly lifts her head up with her hair full of little wisps of ghost mice, and her mother, across the room, shudders and looks away. "Mom, please—help Shelly outside?"

"They're just mice," Grandma says, amused. "Come on, Shelly. Let's get rid of them."

Grandma and Shelly walk out of the house, Shelly's hair writhing with little ghost mice, and Grandma opens the front door so Shelly can step into the yard and comb out her hair with her fingers. It feels good doing the whole job start to finish on her own, especially with her mother there. Usually

Shelly watches or just gets to help out a little, but this time it was all her.

"Those cats earn their keep," Grandma says, as the ghosts scamper into the bushes lining the driveway. "Come on, Shelly. Let's go show your mom the mice are gone."

When they walk back into the living room, Shelly's mom is sitting as far away from the vent in the floor as possible with a cat in her lap.

"All gone," Shelly says. "No more ghosts in your floor, Mrs. Potts."

"Thank you," Mrs. Potts says. "Let me get you some money."

"Oh no," says Grandma. "Edna, don't worry about it. We're friends and you're feeding us dinner. That's more than enough."

Mom glances up, briefly, at the ceiling then looks at Shelly as she takes a seat beside her. Shelly's worried she'll be mad, but she smiles.

"Extra pie for you tonight," she says. "When you fill your hair with dust and mice for your neighbor, you get a big slice and as much ice cream on the side as you want."

Shelly can't help hoping that maybe this means her mom's

coming around to seeing things *her* way—seeing that Shelly isn't just a kid and should be allowed to work with Grandma in the field. She smiles back at her mom. "Really?"

"Really," Mom says, reaching out to give the ends of Shelly's hair a playful tug. "You *do* have to wash your hair when we get home, though. I can see cat hair in it from here."

4

Grandma doesn't get rid of every ghost she comes across. She says sometimes ghosts deserve to do their haunting. And sometimes people deserve to be haunted.

"You don't take ghosts from a graveyard," Grandma says, braiding Shelly's hair so she won't catch any ghosts she doesn't want. "Not unless they want to go, and then you can let them out. Most of those ghosts will leave if they really want to. Same with sacred places, churches and temples. Any ghosts doing their haunting there deserve to stay."

Shelly rolls her eyes. "I know," she says. "Sometimes it's the living who make trouble for the dead."

Grandma snorts, tugging playfully on the end of Shelly's braid. "It's good to know you've been listening."

One of the first places Grandma took Shelly for ghost lessons was a graveyard—an old one where nobody had been buried for years. It was tucked in a small lot between a strip mall and a block of townhouses and kept tidy by the city.

There was a ghost there, a faint shade of a person slowly transitioning from ghost to gone.

"Not everyone can see the dead," Grandma said, pointing to the blurry shape propped up against the chain-link fence. "We can, and that means we've got responsibilities."

Shelly was six and so excited about seeing the ghost she could hardly sleep. Mom decided that meant she was scared, but she wasn't. Even then, she liked the dead.

The graveyard Grandma takes Shelly to this time is a 27-minute bus ride away. It's a modern one—big, with tidy rows of tasteful headstones and brass plaques set in the ground. Shelly keeps to the path so she doesn't walk on anybody's grave.

"This kind of graveyard, you aren't going to find a lot of ghosts," Grandma says, leading Shelly toward the outer limits of the graveyard to the cheaper graves. "Lots of old ladies like me with nothing left to haunt about."

On the outskirts of the graveyard are small graves with tiny aluminum stakes and rusted old plaques instead of proper headstones. They're the cheap seats of burial places for people who can't afford or aren't willing to pay for a big headstone get buried. The graves are closer together and weeds sprout up between them. There's a ghost there, a teen-aged boy, sitting on a small grave, playing with a black plastic box that looks almost like a radio.

He looks up at Grandma and Shelly with eyes like black holes.

"Hello, Joseph," Grandma says, sticking a hand in her purse and pulling out a stack of old cassette tapes. Shelly's mom has a tape deck in her car, but these days tapes are all of old music and hard to find. Grandma puts them on the grave in front of the boy and he smiles at her.

"Old Lady," he says. His mouth moves, but his voice comes from the headphones around his neck. He pops open his ghostly radio-like box and inserts the tapes one by one right after each other. They disappear as they slide into place, dissolving into the player. Ghosts don't usually come with accessories—Joseph having the player and headphones means he was buried with them. "You want to know who's roaming around the yard?"

"First I want to introduce you to my granddaughter," Grandma says. "Joseph, this is Shelly."

Joseph turns his unsettling eyes on Shelly. She does her best not to take a step back. After a moment, she bows to him, just a quick up-and-down bob, because she's not sure what else to do when he's staring like that.

Joseph laughs. "I like her," he says. "Old Lady never introduced me to anyone before, Little Shell. You must be special. You ever heard of The Cure?"

Shelly shakes her head.

Joseph opens his box again and reaches inside. His hand slips down, down, all the way to his elbow as he digs around inside, and he pulls out a cassette and holds it out to Shelly. "They're my favorite band. This is a good tape," he says. "My favorite album. Take care of it for me."

Shelly takes the tape. The faded lettering on it reads *Disintegration*. It's so icy cold that touching it feels like being burned, but Grandma taught her how to accept gifts from the dead. When they give you something, you have to be grateful. You smile, say thank you, and take good care of it.

"Thank you," Shelly says. "Do you want me to bring it back?"

"Nah," Joseph says. "You keep that one for you. I got it memorized. Old Lady here brings me new stuff to listen to all the time."

Shelly slips the tape into her pocket. Joseph isn't as old as most ghosts she's met. She wonders about that, but another thing about ghosts is that it's rude to ask how they died. Most of the time Shelly and Grandma don't even ask ghosts why they're still hanging around when they meet them. Most of the time ghosts don't even know they're ghosts.

Joseph does. He sits on his grave and hums as music starts playing from his headphones. It sounds angry to Shelly—angry and sad. Joseph smiles like he likes it.

"What is that?" Shelly asks, pointing to the box. "It plays tapes?"

"It's a tape deck," Joseph says, his voice filled with pride echoing between the notes of the song. "It's top of the line— the best portable tape deck money can buy. Always wanted one of these when I was alive. This tape was a good choice, Old Lady. You've got depths."

Grandma laughs and takes a seat across from Joseph. She pats the grass beside her for Shelly to sit, too. "I like to think so. You said something about people roaming?"

Joseph makes a face. "Always business," he says. "Yeah, we got some new ghosts. John Francis German over on the north side is confused. Doesn't want to talk much. Estelle K. J. Park called me a punk kid and told me to get off her lawn."

Shelly can't help the laugh that bubbles out of her.

Joseph turns to her, smiling. "Little Shell gets me. Old Lady never laughs at my jokes."

"I'll laugh at your jokes when you get funnier," Grandma says. "Do you think they want to move on? Do you think they need help?"

Joseph shrugs. "They don't seem to like it here much."

They talk to John Francis German first. He's old, but not old-old—in between Shelly's mom and grandma in age. He's dressed in khakis and a polo shirt. He flickers in and out of focus as he wanders the north side of the graveyard, looking around like he's lost.

He smiles when they get his attention.

"Hello," he says politely. "I'm sorry. Could you give me directions? I'm not sure where I am."

"Oh yes," Grandma says, as she lets her hair out of its braid to catch him. "We can show you where you need to go."

John comes with them to find Estelle K. J. Park. She isn't as nice.

"Do you know how much I paid to be here?" Estelle asks, her voice croaky like a frog's. She's wearing a fuzzy bathrobe and big slippers. The lenses of her glasses are fogged over and Shelly can't see her eyes. "I've got a big headstone coming. I ordered one with an angel on it—life-size. I'm not going anywhere until I see my angel."

Estelle turns her back to them and John bends down close to Shelly and whispers, "I don't think she's lost."

Shelly suppresses a laugh. Estelle doesn't seem like the kind of ghost who'd like being laughed at.

"No," Grandma agrees, matching John's tone. "She's exactly where she wants to be."

"Darn tootin'," says Estelle. "I know where I'm going, make no mistake. I didn't take orders from anyone when I was alive and I'm certainly not going to start now I'm dead. I'll move along in my own time."

Grandma smiles at Estelle. "You take your time," she says. "Go when you're ready and let me know if you need help."

"Help!" Estelle scoffs and plants her hands on her hips. "I think I can figure out death on my own."

"You see?" Grandma says, leading Shelly and John away from Estelle's grave. "Ghosts in places like this—they know their business most of the time."

"Are they always that rude?" Shelly asks, looking up at Grandma. Joseph was more interesting than John, who's hooked on the ends of Grandma's hair, and nicer than Estelle. Shelly would rather go back and talk to him more.

"Not usually," says Grandma. "She's a special case."

"I'm sorry?" says John. "Ghosts? Did she say she was dead? Did she—" He pauses and raises his hands, peering at the way they're slightly translucent. Shelly can see the grass and the graves on the other side of him plain as looking through a dirty window. "Oh," he says. "I suppose she did."

Grandma looks at John. "Do you want to stay here?"

"No," he says. "No, I don't think so. I think I want to go. I think I want— They say it's the next great adventure. It's a great mystery, isn't it? That's exciting. You know, it's been a long time since I went somewhere new."

As they walk toward the cemetery gates, John leaves them—going wherever his next, new place is.

"See? There are as many different kinds of ghosts as there are people," says Grandma. "Nobody's life is the same and nobody's death is the same. That's all it boils down to."

It feels bigger than that to Shelly. She knows ghosts, has talked and played with the dead, but whatever comes next, whatever's after ghosts—that looms in her mind whenever someone like John Francis German moves on. Shelly can't help wondering what it's like, what's really there, and why more people don't stay behind.

5

The only cassette player Shelly knows of is the one in her mom's car. Every time they go shopping at the thrift store, Shelly's mom makes a point of looking for tapes, searching for something good. It should be easy to convince her mom to play Joseph's tape, except that Joseph is a ghost and Shelly knows how her mom feels about ghosts.

The next time they go out, just Shelly and her mother, Shelly takes the tape with her. It's warm now—looks and feels just like any other tape, not like a gift from a ghost at all, but Shelly still doesn't work up the courage to ask to play it before they reach the thrift store. Instead she stands there with the tape in her pocket and watches her mother sort through rows of Christmas albums and church music.

"When I was your age I used to sit with my tape deck and record songs off the radio one by one," her mother says.

"I used to call in and request my favorite songs and hover over the tape deck to catch what I wanted when it got played." She squints down at a tape with a picture of a lute on the front of the box then puts it back among the Christmas albums.

"I might have to find a tape deck and start doing that again." The thrift store keeps the box of tapes tucked away in the back corner of the shop and sells each tape for 25 cents. Cheap, because nobody wants them anymore. "Especially if your grandma keeps borrowing the good tapes and *losing* them."

After meeting Joseph at the graveyard, Shelly knows Grandma isn't losing the tapes at all, but she doesn't say so. Grandma and Shelly have ghost secrets, which is only fair, since Mom and Shelly have secrets, too.

"Do you want to see if there's any music you like?" Mom asks, stepping back from the box of tapes. "Or should we give up this week and go get lunch instead?"

Joseph's tape is a heavy presence against Shelly's hip. "I'm okay," she says. "Lunch sounds better."

"Thank God," says her mom. "I'm starving."

• • •

Lunch is Mom and Shelly's secret because Grandma doesn't believe in overcharging for ghosts or paying someone to make food for you. Zhou's Family Restaurant—a Chinese restaurant that does burgers and fries as well as Szechuan American food—is beside the thrift store. When her mom's having an especially good or an especially bad week, they'll get milkshakes and split an order of french fries and sweet and sour pork.

Zhou's is always loud and busy on the weekends—full of families getting lunch and people placing takeout orders—but Shelly and her mom get a two-person table in the back corner of restaurant.

They order their food and Shelly's mom leans back in her chair. Her eyes are tired, but she smiles at Shelly anyway. "One day we're going to have a nicer car. Then we won't have to troll the thrift store for new tapes on the weekends. We'll listen to whatever we want."

Shelly sees her opening and pulls Joseph's tape out of her pocket. "Can we listen to this?" she asks, holding it out to her mother. "It's new."

Her mother takes the tape and turns it over in her hands. "Where did you get it?" she asks. "Why *this* tape?"

Shelly hesitates, but even if her mother doesn't approve of ghosts, there are only so many places Shelly could have gotten a tape. Sometimes it's easier to tell the truth. "One of Grandma's friends gave it to me."

Mom looks up, eyebrows raised. "A dead friend?"

Joseph *is* dead, and technically a dead friend is an accurate description, but it seems rude somehow to focus on the fact that he's no longer alive. "His name is Joseph."

Shelly's mom laughs and tucks the tape into her purse. "Joseph has a strong commitment to theme," she says. "We can listen. I used to like The Cure."

Their milkshakes and food arrive, and Shelly picks up her chopsticks as her mother serves them both from the larger plate. Shelly's never heard of The Cure before, but Joseph wears all black and sits in a graveyard— something even ghosts don't normally do. "You like The Cure?"

"I used to," her mom says, picking up a fry. "When I was the age I'm guessing Joseph is—a teenager?" She waits for Shelly to nod then grins. "I thought so. I was like him, I bet. I had a lot of feelings. I listened to a lot of music." She pauses. "I talked to a lot of ghosts."

Shelly doesn't get to hear her mother talk about ghosts in a way that isn't disapproving very often. "When?" she asks. "You never work with Grandma."

"There's more to life than ghosts, Shelly," she says. "They *seem* interesting, but most of them are broken reflections of who they were when they were alive. Most of them just need a chance to fade on their own. Besides, somebody needs a steady income in this family. There's no telling what kind of magic people will want to see in a month—or a year. Banishing ghosts could go out of fashion."

"People are always going to die," Shelly says, frowning. "There'll never be a shortage of ghosts."

"True," says her mom. "But that doesn't mean we have to be the ones who deal with it. Some people deserve to be haunted—even if it's by the cat of their house's last owner. Sometimes the cat was there first."

Getting rid of a cat sounds like the kind of job Grandma would take. Shelly takes a sip of her milkshake. "Did you meet a cat ghost?"

Shelly's mom laughs. "Shelly, sweetheart, by the time I was your age I'd met *so* many cat ghosts."

In the car on the drive home from the restaurant, her

mom slides Joseph's cassette into the tape deck and fast-forwards through the first song straight to the second.

The music is all jangly guitar, electric piano, and echoing, sorrowful voices. The singer only has pictures left to remember the person he loved and lost. The song sounds like a sad dance party. It's hard to imagine her mom listening to this kind of music, but Shelly likes it. It's . . . haunting.

Shelly's mom might not approve of ghosts or Shelly making friends with Joseph, but she turns the music up, singing slightly off-key. When the song finishes, she rewinds it and starts teaching Shelly the words so she can sing along, too.

6

Two cops knock on their door while Shelly's mom is at work. One of the cops is a stranger—a white guy with close-cropped blond hair—and the other is Jenny, Mrs. Potts's daughter.

"We could use your help down by the river, Louisa," Jenny says. "It'd make this whole thing go a lot faster." The police come to ask Grandma for help sometimes, off the books. Not often, and always with their hats in hand. Jenny's partner looks like he can't quite believe what they're asking.

Grandma looks Jenny and her partner over then nods. "Okay," she says. "Shelly, get my coat and our bus passes."

"Should she be coming with us?" the other officer asks, looking uncomfortable as Shelly helps Grandma into her raincoat.

"She helps me with the ghosts," Grandma says, which doesn't seem to reassure him.

Shelly knows her mom wouldn't let her go if she was home, but she keeps her mouth shut. Going to graveyards and fancy apartments is interesting, but sometimes the only reason Shelly goes with Grandma to deal with the ghosts of people's pets is because it's better than doing homework. This is a different sort of ghost work—this is *exciting* in a way that catching other ghosts isn't. It's more interesting. It means Grandma trusts Shelly to handle more difficult jobs.

Shelly's supposed to go watch a movie at Isabel's today. This is better.

"We can give you a ride," says Jenny. "It'll take a while to get to the river on the bus."

"In the back of your car?"

Jenny pauses. "Well," she says. "Yes."

"No thank you. We'll meet you at the water," Grandma says, her voice so firm that Jenny and her partner have no choice but to leave and drive away as Grandma and Shelly begin walking to the bus.

"Never get in the back of a car with doors you can't open," Grandma tells Shelly, holding her hand as they make their way down the sidewalk. "You be polite to the police, but stay out of that car."

It's a dreary day—gray and damp—and Shelly thinks it would be kind of cool to ride in a police car, even on a day when taking the bus didn't mean wading through puddles, but she doesn't say so. Grandma's got a point about getting in cars with doors you can't unlock.

It takes longer to get to the river by bus than it does to get to the cemetery. When they get there, Jenny has a cardboard cup of tea for Grandma and a fancy hot chocolate for Shelly, which makes the long bus ride worth it.

"We just need help finding him," Jenny says, gesturing out at the river. It's wide and deep and its murky water is deceptively sluggish. "It'd save us a lot of time if you can figure out where he ended up."

Grandma takes a sip of her tea, scanning the river's edge. "We'll see if he's around," she says. "I'll give it a shot." She hands her tea to Shelly and unbraids her hair, letting it hang loose around her shoulders. When she takes her tea back, Shelly starts to let her hair down, too, but Grandma stops her. "Just watch today," she says. "Give me your hand, though. The ground's slippery."

They walk up and down the banks of the river, the cops trailing after them. Grandma's hair blows around her face, ready to pull up any ghosts that cross their path.

The earth is soft and the mud sucks at Shelly's feet. The

hems of her pant legs get heavy with water and dirt. Shelly's been to a lot of haunted places and seen a lot of ghosts, but this is more miserable than any haunted house. Her hot chocolate helps a little, but the drizzling rain and gray skies feel *sad* in a way hauntings don't usually feel to Shelly. Maybe going to Isabel's would have been better after all.

It takes three passes along the river for Grandma to catch the ghost they're looking for. His clothes are soaked, plastered to his body, and his shivering makes him shift in and out of focus. He doesn't speak, but he keeps glancing over his shoulder toward a little outcrop of rocks jutting out into the water.

"Ah," Grandma says, nodding. She gestures the cops closer and points to the rocks. "He's caught up in there. A nice young man with a red beard."

The cops wait until Shelly and Grandma leave to pull the body from the water, but the ghost comes home with them, wet and shivery even after the bus ride back to the house. He doesn't seem to notice the change of scenery much, just stares into the middle distance and lets Grandma pull him along.

"Do you want me to turn on the heater?" Shelly asks, when they get to the house.

The ghost jumps and looks down at her. "Where did you come from?"

"Leave him alone, Shelly," Grandma says, unlocking the door. "We'll feed him and send him off. He doesn't need us confusing him even more."

"I don't understand what happened," the ghost says, bobbing into the kitchen in Grandma's wake. "I was just standing by the water. I was just thinking."

Grandma pours the ghost a mug of milk and warms it in the microwave as he drifts around their kitchen, flickering in and out of focus. Shelly watches, fascinated. A ghost who is still deciding if he wants to stick around or not, a ghost this freshly formed, is new for her.

"What's your name?" Shelly asks because the cops hadn't said.

The ghost turns to face Shelly and gives her a distressed look. "I don't know," he says. "I don't know what happened. Do you know who I am? Do *you* know my name?"

Grandma sets the mug of warm milk down on the kitchen table. "Here you go," she says. "This will warm you up and then we'll make sure you get where you're going. We'll help you get to where you're supposed to be. That sounds nice, doesn't it? Shelly, would you get the scissors from my sewing kit?"

Shelly goes and gets the pair of small silver scissors.

The ghost drinks from his mug of milk. His wet hair drips real water on the floor. He looks like he'll never be fully dry, like if you tried to wring him out he'd twist and twist and the water would just keep coming. It's probably why Grandma doesn't want to keep him around long. Having a damp ghost haunting their house would be troublesome. Mom's *definitely* going to notice the river water all over the kitchen.

Grandma wraps a strand of hair around her ring finger and clips it off. By the time the milk is finished, the ghost is nearly gone, just a faint smudge in the air where once there was a man.

"Where do they go?" Shelly asks, once he's faded fully from view. Shelly has a lot of experience with animals and not a lot with people—definitely not with the ghosts of people Grandma pulled up from somewhere other than a graveyard. Seeing the river ghost leave, not knowing what's next for him or who he was when he was alive, is unsettling. Shelly's only seen human ghosts leave from graveyards before. What happens to ghosts when they move on isn't the interesting part of ghosts to her, but now she can't help wondering. The river ghost didn't know where he was. How could he know where to go from here? "Where do we send them?"

Grandma picks up the mug and refills it with milk. She sticks it in the microwave to heat it up for herself. "I think they're going where they need to be."

Shelly frowns. "You don't know?"

"I don't know everything about ghosts," Grandma says, amused. "We'll find out what comes next one day, but that day's far off in the future. There's no point worrying about it now."

Shelly looks at the empty chair and suppresses a shiver. Ghosts aren't scary. Ghosts, she knows. The future is another thing entirely.

• • •

Mom comes home from work tired, her hair pulled up in a high, tight bun. The water from the ghost is gone, but there's dirt smudged on the floor beneath his chair. Mom takes one look at the dirty linoleum and her exhaustion turns into annoyance.

"Did you bring a ghost home?" she asks Grandma, like Shelly isn't in the kitchen with them helping Grandma make spaghetti for dinner.

"We fed him some milk and sent him on his way," Shelly says. "He wasn't scary. Just confused."

"He moved on peacefully," Grandma agrees. "He just needed some kindness before he left."

"You can't bring the dead home with you," Mom says. "Isn't that what you taught me? Don't let them linger."

"You're misconstruing my lessons." Grandma turns away from the onion she's cutting to tear a sheet off the roll of paper towels sitting on the counter. "Shelly, here. Help your mother with the floor."

Shelly doesn't take the sheet. She doesn't want to be sucked into their argument. If she does, it'll just lead to Mom lecturing her about ghosts again—about how she's going to have bad dreams or how everyone at school is going to think she's weird if she keeps playing with ghosts all the time.

"It's not about the floor," Mom says. "You know it's not about the floor."

"Sometimes people need help. Alive or dead. How do you say no if you can provide it for them?"

"What people?" Mom asks, throwing her hands in the air. "What ghosts? I'm not saying you can't help them, Mom. I'm saying don't bring them into our house and don't take Shelly with you when you go—don't drag her along to deal with strange ghosts. You take all the jobs you want. Charge some money or ask for favors—do whatever you want, Mom. You're an adult. But Shelly doesn't need to grow up with ghosts in her hair and her head."

"I'm teaching Shelly the same things I taught you," Grandma says. "She knows the rules. I don't know why you're so worried. The dead aren't anything to be concerned about."

"*I* find them concerning!"

Shelly slinks out of the kitchen to avoid the rest of the argument. She doesn't want to get caught between her mom and her grandma. She *knows* her mom is just trying to look after her, but that doesn't mean Shelly thinks she's right, and she doesn't want to say that to her face.

Shelly knows where she stands with ghosts, even if her mother doesn't like the work that Shelly and Grandma do. It's important. Even if Shelly's a little worried about where they're sending ghosts *to*, the dead are just people. It's like Grandma says—when someone needs your help, you give it.

7

After Mom and Grandma's argument over the river ghost, it takes a while for Grandma to bring Shelly with her on a job again. Grandma waits until a Saturday when Mom is working late. She knocks on Shelly's bedroom door and says, "How would you like to go downtown today?"

Shelly looks up from the book on parapsychology she got out of the library—it's useless, full of facts about electromagnetic fields, and Shelly is pretty sure those don't apply to ghosts at all. Honestly, it's pretty funny—a whole field of people who think ghost hunting is all infrared cameras and EMF readers are so caught up thinking they know everything that they don't realize they're going about finding ghosts all wrong.

Shelly *would* rather be doing something else, though. "What for?"

"Ghosts," Grandma says, a note of triumph in her voice. "We're going to go someplace *nice*."

Shelly closes the book.

Grandma pulls Shelly's hair back into a neat French braid and ties her own in a bun. She makes Shelly change out of jeans into a skirt. They take the bus all the way into the heart of downtown, to a fancy old hotel, and Grandma leads Shelly through the big lobby to the concierge desk.

"We're here about your ghost," Grandma tells him.

He smiles at her indulgently—like he thinks he knows what Grandma is here to say. "Lots of people stay here hoping to see her," he says. "We sell a book about the history of the haunting if you're interested in more information. I've never personally had an encounter, but I know a few staff members who think they have. I'm not sure I believe in ghosts."

Grandma isn't always *asked* to take jobs and doesn't always get to help the ghosts she comes across. Sometimes the living think they're more important than the dead.

"Oh, you've got a ghost all right," says Grandma. "Could I speak with the hotel manager?"

The concierge pauses, the smile slipping from his face. Grandma's question has obviously caught him off guard. "The manager?" he repeats. "Can I ask what you want to speak to him about, ma'am? He might not be available right now. I could certainly pass on a message for you."

"We can wait until he's free," Grandma says, smiling at the concierge, stubborn as anything. "We want to talk to him about your ghost problem and I could use a cup of tea. I'm sure the restaurant is a perfectly comfortable place for us to wait. Would you call and let him know we're here?"

Grandma stands right where she is, staring the concierge down, until he gives in and reaches for the phone. Shelly feels smug. Grandma can be immovable as a mountain when she wants to be—same with Mom. Maybe that runs in the family the way seeing ghosts does. Shelly hopes so. She wants to be like that, too.

"I'll call," he says. "No promises. I'm not sure—what *about* the ghost?" There's a look in his eyes like he thinks maybe they're going to claim something outlandish, something unbelievable that he's going to have to deal with.

"I'm a professional," says Grandma. "I deal with the dead for a living. I'd like to speak with the manager about helping your ghost move on."

The concierge stares at Grandma, and this time she just smiles at him.

"You know what?" he says. "You're right. The manager

should be the one you talk to. I don't get paid enough to decide whether or not the hotel gets an exorcism."

Shelly presses her lips together to keep from laughing, but Grandma doesn't bother hiding her amusement. "Perfect," she says, grinning at the concierge. "We'll be in the lounge having some tea while we wait."

• • •

Shelly sees the ghost before Grandma does. The two of them are sitting in the restaurant. Grandma has a pot of orange pekoe and Shelly mint. The concierge called the ghost a *her*, but when one of the brass-doored elevators dings and nobody walks out, Shelly looks over and sees a spectral boy peering at her from inside. He looks about her age and he's dressed nicely, but in clothes that look old-fashioned—shorts and a blazer, his socks pulled up to his knees. When a bellhop pulling a cart of luggage walks into the elevator with him, the ghost reaches up and slides a hand over the inside wall.

Shelly can't see inside the car, but the dismayed expression on the bellhop's face and the gleeful look on the ghost's make it pretty easy to guess that he just hit a bunch of buttons.

"Grandma," Shelly says, reaching out to tap her arm, "it's a kid."

Grandma looks up from stirring milk into her tea, following Shelly's gaze to the elevator just as the doors close on the exasperated bellhop. She snorts. "Up to mischief, I see," she says. "You have to respect that in a boy his age—he's keeping himself entertained."

"You mean he's bored," says Shelly, grinning. She'd love to push an entire bank of elevator buttons. Being a ghost has its advantages.

Grandma nods. "The hotel and its ghost story are both old. Got me thinking that if I was the ghost of this place, I'd be just about ready to move on now. There's only so much unfinished business you can cling to. Besides, I'd be bored, wouldn't you?"

Shelly takes a sip of her tea. "I'm already bored of sitting here. Do you think the manager will actually talk to us?"

"*Someone* will come," Grandma says. She's been doing this since before Shelly's mother was Shelly's age. When she says something is going to happen, it's easy to believe her. "They won't want us living in their lobby. Eventually it'll be easier to send someone down than to have us here."

They have to wait, though. So long that a server comes and refills the hot water in both their teapots. Shelly spends the wait watching the ghost. The hotel staff avoid the boy's elevator when they can. There's a whole bank of them to choose from, so if you know which one is haunted, it's easy to avoid. The ghost looks disappointed every time someone doesn't get in with him.

But Grandma is right. After 40 minutes, a man in a neatly pressed suit with an official little name tag and nice hair comes to speak with them. He's carrying a book and smiling—polite but obviously ready to move on fast.

"Hello," he says. "My name is Marc. Nick says you want to talk to someone about our ghost story?"

"Did you know it's wrong?" Shelly asks, doing her best not to point to the elevators. "It's not a woman haunting the hotel, it's a little boy."

Marc pauses, looking down at Shelly then at Grandma. "I brought you a copy of the official history of the hotel," he says and places the book he's carrying on their table. The cover features a photograph of the hotel's roof. It looks *very* official.

Grandma pushes the book to the side. "I'm offering to get rid of your ghost," she says. "I can see he's bothering your guests and staff, and he's been stuck here a long time. He's restless. I can help him move on."

Marc glances at the haunted elevator like he knows exactly what they're talking about then shakes his head. "Thank you, ladies, but we're quite happy with our ghost. Like I said, she's included in the official history." Marc gestures toward the book. "People love coming to see her. It's a fun spot for the tourists."

"If they've never seen a ghost before, they won't see one now," Grandma says. Shelly's never met anyone else who can see ghosts the way her family can. Plenty of people can *feel* them around, but being able to have a conversation with them and move them the way they can is special. "The dead don't decide to make themselves known to you just the one time. It's all or nothing."

Marc's smile is stiff and official. "I see," he says. "We're really not interested in buying an exorcism."

"Oh, no charge," Grandma says. "I just need your permission."

"We're not interested," he says again. "We like having her around."

"It's not a *her*," says Shelly. "It's a little boy. He's not much older than me. That's why he's playing in the elevator. He doesn't have any friends here and he's *bored*."

Marc looks down at Shelly. "Aren't you a little young to be telling ghost stories?" he asks. "Listen, it's better if it's the ghost of a young woman. A child, that's morbid—sad. The death of a young woman is romantic. People enjoy it more."

Shelly's never seen anyone turn down Grandma's offer before. She feels angry at Marc for saying no. Even people who don't really believe her usually don't mind having her walk around a bit, but Nick the concierge watches them from his desk after Marc leaves. Shelly and Grandma leave the restaurant and go home.

On the bus ride, Grandma takes Shelly's hand in hers. "There's nothing romantic about it," she says. She's annoyed. "Death is just death. You understand?"

Shelly didn't like Marc much either, but the boy in the elevator hadn't looked too upset about being stuck in the hotel. Maybe he wasn't ready to move on—some ghosts were stuck, but some wanted to stay. Shelly doesn't like the hotel keeping the ghost around just to make money, doesn't like him having his story changed, but maybe he's happy haunting the elevators.

Grandma's obviously upset about the ghost this time, though, so Shelly can't say it doesn't seem that bad to her. She nods instead. "I know."

Grandma gives Shelly's hand a gentle squeeze and lets go. "We shouldn't tell your mother about this one," she says. "I was hoping for a different outcome, but she'll worry about this."

Shelly's got ghost secrets and french fry secrets. She doesn't want her mother to worry about either. She nods and squeezes Grandma's hand. "I won't tell, I promise."

• • •

The long wait in the hotel lobby means Mom is home from work when Shelly and Grandma open the front door.

"Let me guess," Mom says. "Ghost hunting?" Her hair is loose around her shoulders and she's changed out of her uniform into a hoodie and leggings. "Mom, we *just* had this discussion!"

"We didn't get close to the ghost," Grandma says. "We observed it."

Shelly's mother closes her eyes and breathes in deeply,

exhaling through her nose. "Okay," she says, pulling a hair tie out of her hoodie pocket. She reaches up and twists her hair into a bun. "Shell, we're going to go pick up some food for dinner. Go to the car, please."

The tension between Grandma and Mom is thick in the air. Shelly turns on her heel and walks back out the door. She doesn't want to be caught in the argument just *waiting* to spark between them. Their family has always been just the three of them living together in a small space. Mom and Grandma fighting makes everything uncomfortable, especially because Shelly's usually what they're arguing about.

Mom doesn't take long to follow her out, slamming the door behind her. "We're getting Zhou's," she says. "I need an egg roll."

"We just went to a hotel and had tea," Shelly says, getting into the car. "I didn't even talk to the ghost."

"You should be spending weekends playing with other kids," Mom says, starting up the car. "You should be having friends over, not hanging out in graveyards."

"I like ghosts. I don't mind going places with Grandma."

Mom sighs. "I know you don't," she says, sounding tired. "Promise me you'll have fun too, though, okay?"

It's an easy promise to make. Ghosts can be a lot of fun. "I promise," she says. "Music?"

"You're changing the subject," says her mom, but she's smiling a little, so she's not *too* upset. She reaches out and hits play on the tape deck. Joseph's music fills up the car again, the singer promising some unnamed person, in his thick-with-sorrow voice, that he will always love them.

8

The police come again but not to ask for help. It's late evening this time. Outside it's dark and cold and raining so hard Shelly can hear the water splashing against the house. The cars driving past on the street send huge arcs of water flying through the air.

When Grandma opens the door, Jenny is there, her uniform soggy around the edges like the ghost Shelly and Grandma brought home from the river. She runs her hands through her hair nervously. She glances over Grandma's shoulder, at Shelly, but looks away, focusing on Grandma instead, like she's pretending Shelly isn't there.

"There was an accident," she says. "I'm sorry."

Grandma knows what Jenny means right away. She freezes up in the doorway like someone hit pause. It takes Shelly a little longer.

What Jenny means is the car was so old it could only play tapes. She means the brakes needed replacing. She means

61

the weather was bad and the world was dark. She means Shelly's mother was tired and coming off a long shift. She means there was an accident and Shelly's mom didn't walk away from it.

Grandma comes unstuck gradually, moving slowly as her face crumples. She looks at Shelly—reaches for her—but Shelly can't hear her.

A ringing in Shelly's ears drowns out everything except the sound of her heartbeat, unsteady and too fast. She feels . . . distant. Like she's underwater so she can't see Grandma and Jenny clearly. She can't concentrate on them talking about what happened and how it happened and what to do next. It feels like someone took an ice cream scoop and scooped Shelly out of her body, pulled the part of her that feels things away and set it aside for later.

She walks to her mother's bedroom and sits on her bed. She's there, but she's not. She's there, but it's like she's watching herself. She's watching and she's waiting. She waits and waits. She stays up all night and watches the sun rise through the window.

She waits, but her mother's ghost doesn't come.

AFTER

9

Not everyone who dies becomes a ghost. Most people just move on, but those people don't know about ghosts like Shelly's mom knew about ghosts. They didn't grow up with ghosts clutching at their hair, with a mother who dealt with ghosts for a living. Those people don't have Shelly waiting for them.

Shelly sits in her mother's room all night, waiting for her ghost, surrounded by things that smell like her mom's shampoo—sweet and citrusy, like orange hard candies. Shelly knows ghosts, but it turns out that doesn't mean she knows death. It turns out knowing ghosts doesn't prepare you for the raw ache of missing someone. Grandma was right. There's nothing romantic about death.

When she can't stand to be in the room any longer, Shelly goes looking for her mom. She can't leave the house for long or go very far without her grandma being worried, but she lets her hair out and she circles round and round the neighborhood looking for any sign of her mother. It feels like everything should be different, but it's not. Neighbors walk their dogs. Other kids walk home from school. Shelly passes people jogging who smile and wave hello.

Something should be different, but it's not. The weather is overcast but not raining. People are living their lives. There are no new ghosts to be found.

When Shelly gets back, Grandma is busy arranging things. The funeral. There's a lot of paperwork on this side of death, a lot of money. Mrs. Potts comes over with a tin of cookies and a tuna casserole she sticks in the oven while Grandma's on the phone.

"Do you have anything to wear?" she asks Shelly, and when Shelly shakes her head, Mrs. Potts looks at Grandma. "Why don't I take Shelly shopping tomorrow? We'll find something for her and you won't have to worry about it."

"Would you? That would be a big help," says Grandma. "There's no time to do anything."

"Of course," says Mrs. Potts. She holds out the tin of cookies to Shelly. "What do you think? We'll go to the thrift store and see what they've got."

Shelly wants to say that is where she and her mother

went—that Zhou's Family Restaurant is where they had secret french fries together and Mom talked about one day getting a nicer car—but she presses her lips together and takes a cookie from the tin. "Thank you," she says instead because it's polite and because there are other things Shelly can get at the thrift store.

When they go to the store, Mrs. Potts starts searching for dresses that are black or navy in Shelly's size. Shelly slips away, to the back corner of the store, where the box of barely touched cassettes sits, waiting.

Shelly's never stolen anything before, but tapes are hard to find.

• • •

The dress Mrs. Potts bought is too tight in the collar, but Shelly has other things on her mind the day of the funeral. The service is in a little chapel on the grounds of the graveyard, the same one where they met Joseph. One of Grandma's friends burns sweetgrass and walks around the room, slow and steady, letting them breathe in the smoke.

Shelly sits between Grandma and Mrs. Potts. They're

more comfortable with the ceremony than she is. She tries to follow along as they fan the smoke toward themselves, but she's never been to a funeral before and it's all new. Shelly tries to focus on looking like she knows what she's doing because it's something else to think about. If she's thinking about the scent of sweetgrass, she's not thinking about her mother being dead—she's not thinking about how the next time she sees her, her mom will be a ghost.

Shelly's hair is loose. She has to comb ghosts from it with her fingers on the way to the cemetery, but Grandma doesn't say anything about her hair being down. She understands grief better than most people. Grandma makes her living with the dead, and that means she talks to people who are grieving. That means she's met ghosts who never wanted to die, who were taken from the living too soon. Grandma has helped other people move on before, and now she and Shelly have lost someone, too.

Shelly winds her hair into a loose bun, ready to pull it free if she sees her mother. Grandma wears her hair in braids, wrapped around her head like a crown. They walk hand in hand to the cemetery, where the urn that holds Shelly's mother's remains waits.

Grandma cries as the drummers sing a traveling song to guide Shelly's mother on to her next destination—even though Shelly knows her mom isn't going anywhere yet—and she and Shelly lower the urn into the earth.

Grandma and Shelly step away from the grave. Grandma cries and holds tight to Shelly's hand. They stand and watch until the urn is covered in dirt and the song is done, until the other people at the funeral start coming up to offer their condolences and say how lovely it was—the song, the sweetgrass.

Shelly slips away from all the hugging and touching and walks to the outskirts of the cemetery.

"Little Shell," Joseph says, looking at her with his black, blank eyes and his mouth that moves while his headphones emit the tinny sound of his voice. "Did you bring me a tape?"

"Do you want to learn French?" she asks, pulling her three stolen tapes from her pockets. "The thrift store had these."

Joseph looks offended. "No music?"

"My mom died," Shelly says. "I can't find her."

Joseph reaches for the tapes. He feeds them into his Walkman one by one. "*Je suis désolé*. That means I'm sorry. *I'm* dead. It's not so bad."

"Says you," says Estelle K. J. Park, she and her fogged-over glasses suddenly appearing beside Joseph. "With your Walkman and your constant moping. Young lady, did you know my angel's still not up? It should be up by now!"

Joseph lets out a world-weary sigh. "*Oui, oui—je connais la musique.* Estelle, Shelly's mother just died."

Estelle stops talking and leans back, crossing her arms over her chest. "Well, shoot," she says. "Sorry, kid. What'd you go for on her grave—something classy or something a little *bold* like me? How big's the tombstone?"

Shelly doesn't really want to talk about what her mother's grave is going to look like. She shrugs. "Grandma did that stuff."

"You ask your grandma for me. You tell her, too—you tell her to see about my angel. It's taking too long." Estelle pauses, tilting her head as she looks down at Shelly. "You'll be all right, kid. You'll see her again before you know it. Not like the rest of us. Nobody visits and nobody could see me if they did."

And message delivered about her angel, Estelle is gone and Joseph and Shelly are alone again.

Shelly can feel tears prickling at the corners of her eyes

and words tugging at her throat, trying to worm their way out of her. She swallows them because she won't weep on the dead. There's no rule against it, but she wants to be strong— she wants to seem better at this than she is.

They come out anyway.

"I can't *find* her," she says. "I miss her. I can't remember what her voice sounds like. Not exactly. What if I forget how she smells next?"

Joseph is a ghost, so he doesn't really get what she means. Shelly can see that on his face.

Shelly also doesn't know who else to talk to.

"You're a ghost," she says. "You live here. If you see her—"

"I don't live anywhere," Joseph says. He pauses, nods. "But if I see her, I'll tell her Little Shell is looking for her mother. I'll tell her you want to hear her voice again."

Shelly doesn't think to wonder how Joseph will know it's her mother until after she finds Grandma and the rest of the funeral party getting ready to head back home, where there's lots of food and more people waiting to say how sorry they are—her mom's coworkers and Grandma's clients, their other neighbors. Shelly hadn't realized her mom *knew* this many people. Jenny Potts opens the door to the back seat of her Prius and Shelly crawls in. Shelly lays her head in Grandma's lap and closes her eyes.

Nobody talks as Jenny starts the car. She pulls out of the parking lot and even though Shelly doesn't have a seatbelt on, Jenny doesn't say anything to her about sitting up straight or buckling up. Shelly's mom would have said something.

Shelly watches the telephone wires through the window, black against the mottled gray sky, and thinks about seeing her mother again. "Do ghosts know things?" she asks.

"They know lots of things," Grandma says. "Things they knew when they were alive. All the things they've learned since they died. Ghosts have a lot of time on their hands."

Shelly shakes her head. That's not what she means. "Do they know things about other ghosts? Would a ghost know who another ghost was, before they became a ghost?"

"Ghosts are just like people, Shelly," Grandma says, undoing Shelly's bun and stroking her hair. "They don't have a special connection to other ghosts just because they're all dead."

Grandma cradles Shelly to her chest the way her mom used to when Shelly was small and rubs her back when Shelly starts to cry. "It hurts now, but it's going to be okay," she promises. "I'm here and you're here, and I'm going to take care of you. We're going to be okay."

Okay feels like it's years and years away right now, so far away it might as well be the moon, might as well not exist, but the car keeps driving toward the house and Grandma keeps holding Shelly close. The world keeps moving.

"Your mom loved you very much," Grandma says. "Remember that, Shelly. You were her world. We'll do right by her memory, you and I. You're going to make her so proud."

Maybe she will—maybe she'll get a chance to hear her mother *tell her* she's proud of her. She hasn't come to the house and she wasn't at the cemetery, but that doesn't mean her mother isn't coming. She might be taking her time or caught up in the transition, but Grandma is right. Her mom loves her. She'll come.

Grandma starts humming as she rubs Shelly's back, singing the traveling song from the funeral under her breath, and Shelly falls asleep there, in Grandma's lap, and for the moment things feel just a little bit better.

10

Shelly sleeps in her mother's room instead of her own. Days pass. Grandma doesn't make her go to school, but sometimes they go next door and Shelly gets to play with Mrs. Potts's cats, and sometimes Grandma comes and sleeps in Mom's room with her. The bed feels big and empty, even with Grandma there.

Any day now her mother's going to walk through the door and apologize for being gone for so long, the way she did when she had to pull long shifts at work. Shelly will tell her it's okay. That it doesn't matter if it took a long time, it's just nice to have her home.

Only she doesn't come. They get visits from neighbors and Grandma's clients, and every time someone comes by and it's not her mom, Shelly feels a wrenching in her chest like she's losing her all over again.

Two weeks after the funeral, the visitor is a friend of a friend of Grandma's named Anna. She sits in their kitchen looking nervous and playing with her gold necklace. "I know it's a bad time," she says. "But I think my house is haunted."

Shelly doesn't feel much like dealing with a stranger's ghost right now. The more days that pass without the appearance of her mother's ghost, the more Shelly thinks maybe *home* isn't where her mom thought to appear. But just in case, she doesn't want to be somewhere else when her mom gets here. She lies in bed at night and thinks *tomorrow* and then *maybe next week*. Sometimes she closes her eyes and tries to will her mother's ghost into the house, tries to summon it with just the power of wanting.

It's not *fair*. Her mom should have come back right away. All these other people have ghosts they don't want, and the one time a ghost would make everything *better*, Shelly's mom is nowhere to be seen.

She's coming. Shelly *knows* she's coming, deep down in her bones, but Grandma hasn't ever said anything about ghosts taking so long to show up.

"Shelly, would you make our guest some tea?" Grandma says. Normally she likes meeting new clients, but she sounds tired, like maybe she needs the tea to get through the consultation. She turns to Anna. "We'll have to take a look."

Shelly turns on the electric kettle and gets out mugs for all three of them.

"Thank you," says Anna. "I can pay you. I don't mind. I just want to be sure it's out of my house."

"I think . . . two hundred dollars is our base rate."

Shelly looks over from making tea. "Two hundred?" she asks. They're not *supposed* to charge everyone money—and never before they've seen what the haunting is like.

"A base rate," Grandma repeats. "It may change if the ghost is harder or easier to deal with."

"That's all right," says Anna, looking grateful to be told yes, even if it comes with a steep price. "I'll pay anything."

Anna's house is an old place on top of a hill. Shelly hears the ghost as soon as they step inside—a rattling squeak coming from the fireplace in the living room just off the entrance. The house is huge, with high ceilings and real wood floors. Anna's couches are piled high with decorative pillows, and she has photos of her family all along the wooden mantle of the fireplace.

The sound that fills the living room makes it almost unbearable to stand in. Anna shivers as she leads them inside. Shelly wonders if the noise is as loud for her as it is for Shelly and Grandma or if she can hear anything at all.

"I *see*," says Grandma. "Quite an active ghost, isn't it?"

"So it *is* haunted?" Anna asks, tugging at her necklace. "Sometimes I hear sounds like someone is screaming in here —like someone's being hurt. Can you fix it? Get rid of it?"

"Oh yes," Grandma says. "This won't be a problem at all. The basic package will more than cover it. Shelly?"

Shelly walks over to the rattling fireplace and ducks her head down so she can peer up the dark shaft. She can't see much—it's black with soot and there's no light—but another squeak comes from above her and Shelly is glad her head is up the chimney so no one can see her laugh.

It's an easy ghost. A raccoon that got stuck in the chimney. He looks furious about being stuck. When Shelly lets down her hair, he grabs hold of it eagerly, pulling himself free from the shaft and climbing straight into her arms.

There's still a large part of Shelly that doesn't want to be dealing with someone else's ghost, but she can't help feeling proud when she walks back over to Grandma and Anna. "I got him!"

"That was it?" Anna asks. "I thought there'd be more ceremony."

"He didn't want to haunt you. He just got wedged in the wrong place and couldn't get loose," Shelly says. "He won't bother you again."

"You should get a professional chimney sweep in before you try starting a fire this winter," Grandma adds. "Just in case."

Anna counts out $200 in twenties and Grandma tucks them into her purse. Shelly carries the chittering raccoon out into the daylight and he leaps from her arms, fading from sight as he hits the ground.

Shelly can't help thinking a raccoon isn't worth that much money. "We're not supposed to charge everyone for their ghosts."

Grandma looks down at Shelly. "We're not," she agrees. "Sometimes the rules are what you make of them. Sometimes they need to be bent—broken. Sometimes the world is made of hard choices."

Shelly doesn't like taking the money, but she thinks she knows what Grandma means—that Anna was someone who could afford to pay, and she and Grandma couldn't afford not to charge. That even though Shelly didn't really want to deal with a ghost for someone else, Anna really needed someone to help her get rid of the raccoon stuck in her chimney.

• • •

When they take the bus home from Anna's house, Jenny Potts and her partner are waiting outside their house. Shelly freezes up beside Grandma, her heart rate spiking. Shelly likes Jenny, but she can't help thinking about the night her mom died every time she sees her now. She can't help worrying that there's *more* bad news coming.

"Mom said someone came by for an exorcism." Jenny gives Grandma a sheepish smile. "They beat us to it by an hour."

Grandma raises her eyebrows. "Someone haunting the morgue?"

"No. We need a body found and you— I mean, if it's not too much trouble, Louisa," Jenny says. "I wouldn't ask except nobody can find people as fast as you can."

Grandma takes a long look at Jenny and her silent, vaguely disapproving partner then crosses her arms over her chest. "I'm going to have to charge a consultation fee," she says. "If you want my services."

Jenny and her partner exchange a glance. "A fee?" Jenny

repeats. "We'll have to ask."

"It'll have to be official," her partner agrees. "Something through the department." He looks at Shelly standing in the hallway behind Grandma. "The kind of official that means a crime scene is no place for a child."

Shelly doesn't think she's a child anymore. She's gotten older since her mom died. She can't stop growing up and getting further away from her mom. She frowns at the officer and opens her mouth to tell him she's Grandma's assistant— that just because she's young doesn't mean the dead will scare her or that she doesn't know what she's doing.

Grandma speaks first. "Shelly will stay home this time."

Shelly feels like she just got dunked in cold water. She might not have wanted to help with the raccoon, but she doesn't want to be left out, either. "What?"

Grandma reaches out to touch her shoulder. "Your mother didn't like you going to crime scenes anyway," she says. "You can still come with me to other jobs, Shelly. Just not these ones. Will you be okay by yourself or should I call someone to come and stay with you while I'm gone?"

Shelly scowls. "I'm *fine*," she says. "I'm not a kid."

Grandma looks like she disagrees.

"Mom'll look after you, Shell," Jenny says. "She'd be happy to have you for dinner, you know that. You can play with the cats."

It's like nobody even heard Shelly. Or more likely nobody cares about her opinion. "Okay," she says. "Sure."

Jenny smiles at Shelly and then her attention is back on Grandma, on what Shelly's mom used to refer to as Jenny convincing the RCMP to pay an old Native lady to find bodies for them. Shelly can see, now, why her mom didn't like it. She doesn't want Grandma to go with them, either.

"I'll be back before you know it," Grandma says to Shelly, pressing a kiss on the top of her head. "Mrs. Potts will be happy for you to visit. Don't let her wring any more mouse exterminations from you."

Shelly stands in the driveway and watches Grandma leaving her behind. This time, she gets into the back of the police car when they ask to drive her—breaking another one of her own rules. She waves at Shelly as the car starts and then makes a shooing motion in the direction of Mrs. Potts's half of the duplex.

Shelly waves back until the police car is out of sight then turns around and takes out her key to open the door to their house. She makes herself a peanut butter sandwich for dinner and eats it in the kitchen, alone.

11

Grandma opens the front door all tense—like she's worried Shelly might not be in either side of the house—and although her shoulders relax, she frowns. "Shelly, I thought we agreed you were going to go next door. Edna said you never came over."

"I didn't *want* to go to her place," Shelly says. "I'm not a kid. I don't need a babysitter."

"You don't need to be alone, either," Grandma says. "I'm sorry I had to leave you, Shelly. Rent is going to be due soon. We need the work."

It feels silly for Grandma to say *we* when it's clear she means *her*. Shelly looks down at the parapsychology book she's been trying to read all evening. She didn't find anything useful in it before, but maybe this time she'll find something she missed. Maybe she'll find something that will help her find her mom. She doesn't want to sit with Mrs. Potts and her cats while Grandma works. It just makes her think more about what she's missing. She's tired of feeling sad all the time. She wants to *do* something. Helping with ghosts would be her top choice, but if her grandma's going to cut her off from some of the work, maybe Shelly needs to look elsewhere.

"When can I go back to school?"

Grandma gives her a surprised look. "Do you *want* to go back? You can go back whenever you want to."

Shelly's not entirely sure she wants to go, but right now school sounds better than home. It's something to distract her from the way she feels, like she's a ghost in her own home, waiting for something to happen.

"Yeah," she says. "I want to go back."

"I'll call the school tomorrow," Grandma says. "I'll ask them about Monday."

• • •

Shelly sits in her own bedroom and listens to the call— Grandma talks about Shelly wanting to get out of the house and get her mind off things. She tells whoever's on the other end—the principal or Ms. Flores, Shelly assumes—that she'll be home and they can call if Shelly needs to leave early.

She tells Shelly, too, on the bus to school Monday morning. Shelly's in sixth grade. She doesn't *need* Grandma to come with her to school in the morning, but she'd insisted on taking her. "You don't need to push yourself, Shelly. You can go to the office and tell them you want to call me. I'll come get you."

"I'm okay," Shelly says. "I'll be okay."

"But if you're not, for any reason—"

"I'll call!" Shelly stands up as soon as the bus reaches her stop. "I'll be okay, Grandma. I know how to use a phone."

Shelly wouldn't have gotten away with snapping before. Her mother would've said, *Shell, what's that tone of voice?* and *Don't speak to your grandma like that.*

Her mom can correct her when she comes back.

"Okay," Grandma says, getting to her feet, too. "As long as you know, that's all I ask."

Grandma walks her into the school and to her classroom. Ms. Flores's face creases into a mask of sympathy and sorrow as soon as she sees them. "Shelly," she says. "It's so good to have you back with us today. How are you feeling?"

Shelly feels like the answer to Ms. Flores's question is

obvious, but she lies because she knows the *right* answer. "I'm okay."

"Good," says Ms. Flores. "Do you want to put your stuff away while I talk to your grandma?"

Grandma squeezes Shelly's hand. "Remember," she says, "you don't have to stay for the whole day."

"I'll be fine," Shelly says, pulling her hand away and pretending she doesn't see the concern on Grandma's face. Shelly walks to her desk, nestled in a cluster of four desks, and takes a seat, ignoring her classmates and the way most of them are staring. Lucas, in the desk across from Shelly's, is looking anywhere but at her. Their seating assignments, the layout of the classroom—it's all exactly the same as it was the last time she was here, but Shelly feels like a different person looking at it.

Shelly has no idea what they're studying in class today. Her last day at school feels like it happened months and months ago, not just a few weeks. Shelly's life has become a *before* and an *after* and she doesn't know how to bring them together. It's like being a ghost—she can see all the parts of her previous life, but it doesn't *belong* to her anymore.

Shelly pulls out her pencil case and concentrates on it

because needing a pencil is one thing she can count on not having changed.

"Shelly, you're back?"

It's Isabel. She's playing with the ends of her long hair. She doesn't look unhappy to see Shelly, but she doesn't look happy either—she looks uncomfortable.

"Yeah," Shelly says. "I'm back."

"I heard about— Sorry about your mom," Isabel says. "Ms. Flores had us all make a card. Did you get it?"

Shelly doesn't know. There are a lot of cards stacked up in the kitchen. "Probably. I haven't read them all."

"Oh," says Isabel. "Okay."

Isabel sits at her desk next to Shelly's, gingerly, like she's afraid the chair will collapse under her if she's not careful. The rest of the day is pretty much the same. Shelly sits at her desk and goes out to the playground and it's like there's a bubble around her keeping everyone else away. It's like everyone knows she's there, but they don't want to look right at her.

It's like she's a ghost.

Isabel keeps turning to Shelly and stopping right before saying something. By lunchtime, Shelly wants to tell Isabel to just say whatever she wants to say. She wants to climb up on the jungle gym and yell at everyone that it's not like they'll catch having a dead mom if they talk to her. It's not a *cold*.

Shelly'd probably get in trouble if she did that. Maybe not *trouble*-trouble, but the school would make her sit in the office and they'd call her Grandma to come take her home.

Shelly's mom would laugh and say, *Well, she's not wrong.* Shelly hasn't gotten in trouble at school often, but when she was in first grade Lucas cut off the end of her braid and when she hit him the principal said they were both wrong and called their parents.

Shelly's mom said she didn't see how her daughter hitting a kid after he cut her hair was an unreasonable response. She'd said she hoped Lucas learned his lesson. Then she took Shelly to Zhou's.

"Hitting people shouldn't be your first response," she said, pointing a fry at Shelly. "But fighting back when someone tries to bully you isn't a *bad* thing, Shell. I want you to know it's okay to stand up for yourself." She paused, pushing the plate of sweet and sour pork and french fries toward Shelly. "Let's not tell your grandma everything, though, okay? She doesn't need to know about the hitting or the fries."

Shelly suddenly doesn't want to be at school anymore, but she doesn't want to go home either. She wants french fries and sweet and sour pork and a milkshake. And maybe, if she's honest, Shelly wants to see if her mother is waiting there for her.

There's a whole bunch of places her mom might anchor herself, and maybe Zhou's is unlikely, but Shelly's mom loved the food and it was *their* place. Grandma didn't know about it.

Shelly sits through the rest of the school day and doesn't pay attention to Isabel beside her or Ms. Flores at the front of the room. She sits and she thinks about how she's going to get to Zhou's. She can't ask outright. It would mean giving up her mother's secret and she doesn't want that—it was theirs and it should *stay* theirs.

Still, when her grandma shows up to take Shelly home at the end of the day, Shelly's plan isn't much better. "Can we go to the thrift store on the way home?" she asks. "I don't need to buy anything. I just—want to go." She pauses. "Mom and I used to go there."

Grandma hesitates and for a moment Shelly thinks she's going to have to tell Grandma everything, but then she nods. "Maybe we can find some tapes to take to Joseph."

"Maybe," Shelly agrees, although she has no intention of looking.

The store is on the same bus route as the one they take to get home. Shelly pushes the button for their stop and she and Grandma exit the bus. There are cars outside of Zhou's already—people getting an early dinner or a late lunch. Shelly watches a woman about her mother's age disappear inside as she and Grandma walk past the restaurant and into the thrift store.

"Where did you want to look?" Grandma asks her. "Tapes?"

Shelly shakes her head. There are shelves of books on the opposite side of the store from the tapes. "I'm going to look at books," she says. "You can look at the tapes, though."

Grandma looks around the mostly empty store and considers this. "All right," she says. "It shouldn't take me long to see if there's anything Joseph would like."

It shouldn't take Shelly long to see if her mother's at Zhou's, either. She heads to the book section, stopping as soon as she has a shelf to hide behind, and waits until she's sure Grandma's not looking. Then she leaves the shop, jogs to Zhou's, and pulls open the door, stepping inside.

The restaurant smells comforting and familiar, like fried meat. Shelly's instantly transported back to sharing milkshakes and fries and pork with her mom. She gets a sudden, intense craving for Chinese food, stomach gurgling even though she's not hungry.

The lady behind the counter smiles at Shelly. "Hello," she says. "Are you here for pickup?"

Shelly scans the restaurant for any sign of her mom. There's a rubber bin of dirty dishes on their usual two-person table. The kitchen is noisy, but the restaurant itself is pretty empty. Shelly's spent hours building this up in her head, hours telling herself *maybe*—that Zhou's was a secret just between them, so there was a chance.

Only there's no hint of the dead in Zhou's. It's just a nice family restaurant and Shelly shouldn't have pinned her hopes on this one thing.

Shelly looks at the lady behind the counter and shakes her head. "No," she says, around the lump forming in her throat. "I'm just looking for my mom, but she's not here. Sorry to bother you."

Shelly swallows her tears on the way back to the thrift store. She slips inside and heads toward the back corner where the tapes are kept.

Grandma meets her halfway. "No luck?" she says. "Me neither—nothing Joseph would like. It's all classical and country."

"Let's go home," Shelly says. "I want to go home."

"Of course," says Grandma, sighing and putting a hand on Shelly's shoulder, squeezing gently. She keeps doing that now, holding Shelly's hand or touching her shoulder, like she's worried Shelly is going to run away on her.

Shelly is disappointed, yeah, but she's *frustrated*, too. She'd known Zhou's was a long shot—why would it be more important to her mother than any other place she could reappear? The house or the cemetery makes way more sense and one of those places is already crossed off the list. If she were going to appear at home, she would have done it by now.

So she must be somewhere else.

She'll check the cemetery again. Sometimes the dead are confused when they come back—like John Francis German and the river ghost. They don't know who they are. If her mom's lost, it's up to Shelly to find her.

She already asked Joseph to look out for her mom. She can recruit other ghosts, too. Shelly knows the chances of finding a ghost who's seen her mom are slim, but if there's even a slight possibility—and she's sure there is—then it's worth trying.

She'll find ghosts and ask them if they've seen her mom. She'll show them a photo so they know who to look for. She'll ask if they've run across a woman looking for her daughter.

Her mom is out there somewhere, and Shelly knows just where to start her search.

12

Shelly waits until Grandma starts cooking dinner then goes into her mother's room.

There's a framed photo of Shelly and her mom sitting on the bedside table. It was taken when Shelly was little, but not so little that Shelly can't recognize herself. Shelly's mother is holding her and smiling at the camera. Shelly looks thrilled to be caught up in her mother's arms. The frame is fancy— colored gold with lots of little flowers carved into the metal.

For as long as Shelly can remember, their family was always her, her mom, and Grandma. She doesn't remember the day the photo was taken, but she wishes she could go back. It's a sunny day and they're outside in a park somewhere. Shelly's mom's hair is short, barely reaching chin length. Even if her mom had wanted to, she couldn't have caught ghosts with hair that short. She's wearing a sweatshirt that Shelly recognizes— it's dark red with flowers stitched across the front. Her mom used to wear it all the time. Shelly doesn't know where it went.

Shelly's hands are shaking when she opens up the back of the frame and slips the photo out.

Not going along with Grandma's idea to look at tapes was a mistake, but Shelly hadn't had a plan then. The only cassettes Shelly has left are the holiday ones her mom refused to keep in the car year-round. There are three tucked away in the drawer of the bedside table. Giving one away hurts, but if Joseph has seen or heard anything from her mom, it'll be worth it.

Shelly waits for Grandma to take another job that leaves Shelly home alone, but she doesn't. Instead, Grandma takes the bus with Shelly to school in the mornings, and on days when she doesn't pick Shelly up, Grandma is always waiting with a snack at home, ready to ask about her day.

"What about money?" Shelly asks, the fifth day in a row she comes home to a warm house. Grandma is roasting a pork loin in the oven and the fridge is fully stocked with milk, like Grandma is expecting to feed more ghosts soon. "What about jobs?"

"I'm working during the day," Grandma says. "I shouldn't be leaving you home alone. People who want a ghost out of their house badly enough will accommodate me working daytime hours now."

It's true that people will bend over backward to get rid of the things they don't want. They'll use their vacation days to watch Grandma wander through their homes, plucking up the skittering ghosts of rats and freeing them in the garden.

It's true, but it's another way Grandma is breaking her own rules.

"They'll do anything to get rid of a ghost once they know they have one," Shelly says. "That doesn't mean we should *make* them."

"No," Grandma agrees. "But right now the two of us being together is more important."

Shelly wants to snap at Grandma—to remind her that *she's* the one who left Shelly while she worked with the police in the first place—but she stays silent. She has her tape chosen and a plan in mind, but she can't count on Grandma leaving her alone again anytime soon. It means she needs to sneak out when she knows Grandma isn't likely to check on her. It means going to the graveyard at night.

• • •

Shelly waits until she's sure Grandma is asleep—until almost midnight—and slips out of her bedroom. Shelly's never left the house alone after dark before. She puts on her coat and boots as quietly as she can. The cassette is in her pocket. The sound of the door opening seems much, much louder than she's used to when she turns the lock and pulls it open, but Grandma doesn't stir—just gently snores.

She closes the front door and waits. Grandma doesn't come running out behind her. Mrs. Potts's lights stay off. Nobody is going to stop her from leaving. Even the front yard looks different at night, cast in unfamiliar shadows.

Shelly shivers, alone in the dark, and tugs her coat tighter around her body.

The bus stops running after nine, which means she has to walk to the cemetery. Shelly isn't afraid of the dead, but the unnatural yellow glow of the streetlights makes the night seem scary, like something bad could be waiting for her around every corner. She takes a step toward the road, moving slowly, letting her eyes adjust to the dark.

The night is noisier than Shelly expected. The trees rustle. There are cars on the road. Dogs barking. Shelly's not alone, but she *feels* like she is. Stepping onto the street and starting the long, cold walk to the graveyard, Shelly feels like she's the only person in an unreal world. She has to keep checking street signs to make sure she's going the right way. Everything looks different even though she knows it shouldn't.

She wonders if this is what being a ghost is like. Scary. Confusing. Shelly can see why her mom got lost if it is. Shelly feels like there's something dark lurking around every corner. Like every time the wind rustles a bush, it's someone sneaking up on her.

She can't believe she has to walk *home* after this, too.

When she reaches the cemetery, the gate is closed but not locked. It's easy to push it open and step inside. Surrounded by death, a dozen lingering souls tugging at the ends of Shelly's ponytail, she lets her shoulders relax and her eyes adjust to the darkness. After all this time, and with all she knows, being here is almost like being home.

Shelly tucks her ponytail into the collar of her jacket and begins the trek across the cemetery toward Joseph's grave. She doesn't know if he'll like her tape, but he seemed sorry for her before. She figures he might forgive it being Christmas music.

When she reaches the outskirts of the graveyard, Joseph is there, where he always is, sitting on his grave. He's singing under his breath and looking up at the sky with his eyes like black holes.

"Joseph."

He turns to look at her, eyebrows raised in surprise. "Little Shell," he says. "I don't think you're supposed to be here right now."

Shelly frowns and digs the tape out of her pocket, holding it out to him. "I'm here to ask you if you've seen my mother," she says. "This is the only thing I could find to bring you."

Joseph glances down at the cassette, and for a long moment his only reaction is the buzz of static from the headphones around his neck. Then he looks up at her like he can't believe *this* is what Shelly has to offer. "Christmas carols?"

"Holiday favorites!" Shelly steps closer to Joseph, hand still outstretched. She *needs* this. "It's not *just* Christmas music. There are a couple Hanukkah songs."

"It's not even winter yet." Joseph doesn't reach for the tape. "You gave me three tapes last time. Let's call that a down payment. I don't want what you've got to offer, but I like you. I'd like to help." He tilts his head. "Besides, you want to know if I've seen your mother."

Shelly nods, impatient. "She hasn't come home yet."

"I don't need tapes for that, Little Shell. It's yours for free. I haven't seen her," Joseph says. "Nobody new is out walking. The only real company I've got right now is Angel Lady. Everyone else is fading away."

Estelle is there, suddenly, standing behind Joseph and frowning down at him. "Angel Lady," she scoffs. "As if I hadn't introduced myself. I'm perfectly polite and *this* is the thanks I get. Teenagers."

"I've been here longer than you," Joseph says. "I don't know why you gotta act like you know more about everything than everyone."

"*Teenagers*," Estelle repeats, and then turns her attention to Shelly. "Poor girl, missing your mother. Let me show you my angel. It'll make you feel better."

Shelly doesn't really want to look at Estelle's angel, but she doesn't want to be rude and Joseph is no help to her right now. "Thank you," she says. "I'd love to see it."

Estelle's fogged-over glasses aren't quite solid, but they gleam in the moonlight as she grins at Shelly. "I knew I liked you, kid," she says. "It's *beautiful*. You can't miss it. One of the biggest tombstones in the whole cemetery. I've checked."

"Little Shell," says Joseph, before Shelly can leave to follow Estelle. "You're not dead yet."

Shelly shivers. She likes Joseph, but she doesn't like the *yet*. "I know."

Joseph shrugs. "Just wanted to be sure you did. I like you. Don't want to watch you fade away." He slides his headphones on and leans back to look at the sky again.

Shelly turns away and follows Estelle. Estelle doesn't mind moving over graves and cutting corners, but Shelly sticks to the paths. She keeps her hair to herself all the way to Estelle's grave.

"See?" says Estelle. "My *angel*."

It is a *very* large marker—the angel alone is at least five feet tall and the base it's sitting on adds a couple more feet to its final height. Its wings are half-unfurled, and it looks down at Shelly and Estelle beside her, the expression on its face stern, but gentle. It holds a banner with ESTELLE K. J. PARK written on it.

"It's nice," says Shelly, because she's not sure what else to say. "Big."

Estelle preens. "It's perfect. Exactly what I wanted."

Shelly remembers when Estelle told Grandma she wouldn't leave until she saw her angel. "What are you going to do now?"

Estelle pauses. Her face is turned toward the statue. "I don't know," she says. "This was all I wanted. To make sure they did right by me. Set it up proper. There's no telling with kids these days."

The angel is at least twice as tall as Shelly. "I don't think kids set up your headstone."

Estelle snorts. "You're all kids to me." She reaches up to pat the banner in the angel's hands. "I guess this is the end of the line. Time to go."

Shelly should let Estelle go wherever the dead do when they move on. She should give Estelle the final nudge she needs to go into the unknown.

That's what Shelly *should* do. Joseph said he didn't want to see Shelly fade away. Shelly's not sure she wants to make Estelle fade yet, either. Who knows what's waiting for her on the other side.

"You don't have to go if you don't want to," she says, reaching back to free her hair from her ponytail. "You could come with me instead."

Estelle turns away from her statue, looking Shelly over. Grandma never explicitly told Shelly not to invite a ghost to stay past their time, but it's such a breach of usual practice that Shelly *knows* she's not supposed to make the offer. It's obviously against the rules.

Estelle doesn't know the rules, though, and Shelly gets the impression she wouldn't care much about them if she did. "Why not?" she says. "I'm dead. It's not like I've got a lot going on."

13

Shelly carries Estelle back to the house tangled up in her hair. Having Estelle with her for the walk makes it less scary— the cold weight of another person's soul traveling with her the whole way home is comforting, even if Estelle doesn't talk too much. Ghosts tend to be disoriented when you move them from a place they've gotten used to. Estelle had been in the cemetery long enough to settle in.

The house is still dark when they get home. Shelly slides her key into the lock and opens the door slowly, trying not to make too much noise. Grandma stays asleep through Shelly locking the door, taking off her shoes and coat, and sneaking back down the hallway to her bedroom.

Shelly brushes Estelle out of her hair and looks at the new spirit haunting her room. "You can't let my grandma know you're here," she says. "If she finds out, she'll make you move on."

"When I move on, I'm going to be with the angels. I'm

not afraid," Estelle says, peering around Shelly's room. She talks a big game, but Shelly's pretty sure she's nervous about crossing over. Why wouldn't she be? Nobody knows what's on the other side. Not Grandma or Shelly or even Joseph, who's been dead for a while now.

"Well, until you're ready, you should keep quiet," Shelly says. "Grandma will make you leave right away."

"I can keep quiet, kid," Estelle promises. "I know how to keep a secret. Shouldn't you be sleeping? Isn't it past your bedtime?"

It is. It's almost two in the morning and Shelly's tired from running around in the dark and bringing Estelle home, but she feels like she should be a good host. "I don't have to sleep if you want company," she says. "I can show you around the house for when you're here by yourself."

"It's a small house," says Estelle. "I think I can figure it out. Sleep, kid. You look exhausted. You look like me two weeks before I dropped dead, and trust me—I was tired."

Shelly *does* feel dead on her feet. "Are you sure?"

Estelle shrugs. "I've got nothing but time. You on the other hand still need to get through the business of living. Enjoy it. Being dead isn't all it's cracked up to be. It's a lot like being alive, except when you're dead and people ignore you, you know it's not just because they're rude."

Shelly laughs and climbs into bed. "Lots of people wish they could see ghosts," she says. "They'd pay attention to you if they could."

"Oh, I'm sure they *think* they would. If they could see me, I'd be old hat in a week. TV made me think being a ghost was more exciting than this."

"TV gets most things about ghosts wrong," says Shelly. "Trust me, you'd like it less if they were right."

Joseph didn't go along with her plan the way she thought he would—but things are still working out. Having Estelle in her room is nice. It's not her mother's ghost, but it's company. It's *practice* for when Shelly does find her mom and brings her home for good.

• • •

Shelly and Grandma eat cereal together in the morning and Grandma gives no hint of knowing that Shelly went out or that she brought a ghost back with her. Shelly feels like evidence of Estelle is written all over her face—

like Grandma should take one look at her and just *know*.

But Grandma is distracted, poring over a list of jobs written on the back of a receipt. "I should get a planner," she says. "Your mother was good at keeping track of her shifts. I think I've got a job at two, but I should still be home before school ends."

Shelly prods soggy cornflakes with her spoon and tries not to think about Grandma and Estelle home alone together. "If you wait, I can go with you after school."

Grandma looks up from her scribbled notes. Shelly can see the refusal in her eyes before Grandma even opens her mouth.

"You're the one who told me I needed to know how to look after the dead," Shelly says, before Grandma can speak.

"And you do," says Grandma. "But you need to know how to look after yourself, too."

Shelly knows how to look after herself just fine.

"I'm done," she says, pushing her cereal bowl away and standing up. "I'm going to finish getting ready."

Grandma calls after her when she leaves, but Shelly ignores her. She goes to her room and shuts the door firmly, leaning back against it.

"Have you got any crossword puzzles?" Estelle asks, adjusting the belt on her fuzzy bathrobe. "Or the *TV Guide*? You've got to have something to do around here that isn't sitting and staring at the animals you've got plastered on the walls. I'm bored and the only books you've got are for kids."

"*I'm* a kid," Shelly says, though she hasn't felt like one lately and hasn't wanted to read much either.

Estelle waves a hand like she thinks Shelly's age shouldn't affect the reading material available to her. "I need something to do," she says. "I thought this would be more interesting than the cemetery, but it's more of the same—nothing to do."

"I'm stuck here, too," says Shelly. "Grandma won't let me go ghost hunting anymore."

"Smart lady, your grandma." Estelle's smile has a mean edge to it. "If I were her, I wouldn't want my granddaughter wandering around with ghosts either. I'd want her to have real, human friends. Ones with beating hearts and warm blood who wouldn't give her nightmares."

"I'm not scared of ghosts," Shelly says firmly. "What's to be scared of? All you are is dead."

"As a doornail," Estelle agrees. "It's boring as all get-out on this side of things. Come on, kid. Find me a crossword. Just a couple of puzzles to keep me entertained. I'm going to be here all day with nothing to do otherwise."

"I'll bring you something later." Shelly picks up her backpack. "You need to stay in here. My grandma's going to be home and if she sees you, she'll try to convince you to move on to the other side."

"I'll stay hidden and keep quiet," Estelle promises. "You just make sure you bring me something to entertain myself with tomorrow."

You're not supposed to take ghosts from graveyards. You're not supposed to keep them around when it's time for them to move on. Estelle should be fading away, except Shelly's clinging to her now. Shelly's keeping her locked away, haunting her bedroom. But Grandma—with her fees and her ban on Shelly going with her to learn more about their work—is also breaking rules. So if the rules don't apply to Grandma anymore, why should Shelly follow them?

Ghosts are just part of life. They don't scare Shelly, but what comes *after* ghosts is different. She doesn't know what comes next—she doesn't know where Estelle would go if Shelly helped her on her way. For all Grandma's an expert at ghosts, even *she* can't say what's waiting on the other side.

Being a ghost is better than leaving everything you know behind. Estelle being bored in Shelly's room is better than Estelle not *being* at all. Shelly's just doing what Grandma always said they're supposed to do—she's helping.

14

The cat happens because Shelly sees it on her way home from school. It reminds her of the mice that haunted Mrs. Potts's house. It's a wispy thing—more the suggestion of a cat than anything else—but when Shelly approaches it, holding out her hand and clucking her tongue, it meows and lets her pet it. Touching its fur feels like running her hands over a snow bank, prickly and cold against her palm. Shelly can't help the shiver that runs through her, but the cat is happy to be noticed and even happier to be petted.

Shelly's mom always said no when Shelly asked for a pet before. If she still feels the same about pets now that she's dead, she can put her foot down when Shelly finds her and brings her home.

Shelly unbraids her hair and bundles the ghost into it, winding the cat up in the long strands and tucking it away inside her shirt. Maybe Grandma won't notice she's bringing a ghost—*another* ghost—into the house.

Grandma is in the kitchen, frying fish at the stove, when Shelly arrives. "I'm home," Shelly says, not stopping as she heads to her room. "I have some homework."

"Dinner will be done soon," says Grandma, flipping fish in the pan. It's early, but Grandma likes to eat early. "Fried fish with rice and peas—No Frills had a special on. Wash up and come eat, and then do your homework."

"Okay!" Shelly calls back, wondering if ghost cats would hunt ghost fish.

She pushes open her bedroom door and makes sure it's shut tight before reaching for the comb on her dresser so she can free the cat from her hair. It lands on the carpet just as Estelle pokes her head out of the closet.

"What's that?" Estelle asks. "A cat?"

Shelly raises a finger to her lips. "We can't talk too loud," she says. "Grandma might hear. I thought you could use some company. It's cute, isn't it?"

Estelle and the cat eye each other with equal wariness.

"A cat's not exactly a crossword puzzle," Estelle says, as the cat begins to circle the room, investigating. "A cat's a responsibility."

"It's a ghost cat," says Shelly. "It can't die a second time."

Estelle lets out a throaty cackle of a laugh that startles both Shelly and the cat. "You're right. There are worse starter pets to have. *I'm* not going to take care of this thing on my own, though. I'm not a cat person. I like dogs."

Shelly reaches down to pet the cat and it meows at her. It sounds like it's meowing from the other end of a long hallway. Shelly smiles at the cat and its edges blur even further as it starts to purr, its whole being vibrating.

"Okay," Shelly says, an idea forming in the back of her mind as the cat crawls onto her lap. "That's fine. I like dogs, too."

"Shelly!" Grandma calls from the kitchen. "Dinner!"

Shelly leaves Estelle and the cat. She can tell she was just playing with a ghost. The chill that follows the dead lingers on her skin.

Grandma looks up from plating the fish and frowns. Shelly freezes. Grandma's more sensitive than she is, even if she missed Shelly bringing Estelle home. "Shelly," she says. "You've been around ghosts."

Shelly could lie and try to turn this back on her grandma, who has cobwebs in her gray hair and looks tired, the same way Shelly's mom used to when she came home and made dinner after working all day. She could say Grandma's just confused. Bending the truth seems more practical.

"I went to the graveyard," she says. "I talked to Joseph."

Grandma gives her a sad look, setting her skillet back down on the stove. "Shelly, I'd like to see her, too, but your mother isn't—"

"I just went to see Joseph!" Shelly insists. "I like him."

Grandma pulls out her chair and takes a seat. The kitchen table always feels empty now. "I'm sure Joseph likes you, too, but Shelly, the graveyard is a long way away. You need to tell me where you're going. You have to *ask* if you're going that far on your own."

Shelly looks away. She doesn't like lying and she doesn't like going behind Grandma's back, but she's on a mission. "Sorry," she says. "I'll ask next time."

"Maybe next time we can go together," Grandma offers. "I'm sure Joseph enjoyed your visit. He likes company. Do you want to hear about the job I did today?"

Shelly doesn't, but she nods because maybe it'll distract Grandma until the ghost fades from Shelly's skin, and Grandma tells her about the old house that needed to be cleared of all sorts of small ghosts, rats and mice and spiders.

"The family was very grateful," she says. "They tried to tip, but I couldn't bring myself to accept that. I didn't tell them what was haunting them. They didn't seem like spider people." Grandma laughs. "Their dog kept barking at the rats. They were certain it was the ghost of some kind of axe murderer come to get them in their sleep."

Normally Shelly would laugh, too, but she hasn't felt as much like laughing lately. Especially since Grandma's even keeping her away from normal jobs now, things she wouldn't have thought twice about bringing Shelly along to before her mom died. It's not like there are that many axe murderers out there, but everyone always thinks that's what they're being haunted by—axe murderers or their victims. Nobody wants to admit that death is something that eventually happens to everyone. Shelly understands that better now than she did before. The idea that her mom could be trapped somewhere else, with people who think she's scary, who misunderstand her the way everyone always misunderstands ghosts, hurts so much she can hardly swallow the rest of her fish.

• • •

The cat was unintentional, but Shelly goes looking for the dog. Estelle needs something to do during the day—some company—and the dog can be a friend for the cat, too. Shelly takes a winding route home from school each day, scanning the sidewalks and the streets, and on the fourth day she finds it.

The dog is big, but its bark is like the cat's meow—it sounds like an echo coming from far away. It's friendly. Shelly winds her hair around its neck like a leash and walks it back to the house. The dog is harder to smuggle inside. Shelly crosses her fingers and opens the door as quietly as possible. The smell of roasting meat hits her right away. The dog sniffs the air curiously, tail wagging.

Grandma isn't in the kitchen, though—Mrs. Potts is. She turns and smiles at Shelly. "Your grandma asked me to come over and cook dinner," she says. "Jenny asked her to take a look at a case. We'll all have dinner together. Pot roast should be done in a couple hours. How was school, dear?"

Shelly is grateful Grandma's not home but mad, too— mad Grandma didn't tell her, mad she's been left out again.

"It was fine," she says, keeping a firm hold of the dog. With Mrs. Potts standing right there she can't exactly tell the dog he can't *eat* anymore.

It licks her cheek, its tongue icy on her skin like getting hit with a splash of cold water. Shelly has to grit her teeth to keep from reacting so Mrs. Potts doesn't think something strange is going on.

"How long until Grandma's home?"

"Not long," says Mrs. Potts. "Would you like me to—"

"Homework!" Shelly says, and heads toward her room, tugging the dog along with her.

When she gets to her room, Estelle is sitting on the bed with the cat in her lap. Shelly pulls the dog inside and shuts the door.

"A dog is *still* not a crossword puzzle." Estelle lets the cat off her lap and gets to her feet so the dog can sniff her hand. "You're going to crowd us out of your room, kid, make it hard to stay. If you're bringing more ghosts in, could you at least bring me someone I could talk to? Someone who can hold up their end of the conversation."

"I'll think about it." Shelly kicks a pile of clothes aside on the way to her bed then throws herself onto it.

The dog and the cat and even Estelle are like a test. Can Grandma tell she's been gathering ghosts? Will she say something? If so, when? What's the limit? Will she come and clear the dead from Shelly's bedroom even though Shelly wants them?

Shelly feels like the fingerprints of the dead are all over her, like everyone should be able to tell, just by looking at her, that she's different. That she's marked by them, becoming one of them. Except if she were a ghost, Grandma would *have* to pay attention to her. So far, nobody's noticed, or at least nobody cares, that she's collecting ghosts in her room. They should. Somebody should say something. Should stop being so distracted by bills and clients and work and *see her*.

When Grandma and Jenny make it back home, they both look tired. Grandma smiles at Shelly and presses a kiss to her forehead. "Sorry," Grandma says. "I feel like I've been drowning in the dead."

Shelly gives Grandma her best smile and then she lies to her face. "Don't worry. Everything's fine."

15

The next day goes by slowly. Shelly is more focused on the ghosts slowly piling up in her bedroom and on finding her mom than on school. School is a place she has to go during the day, but she sits quietly and does her homework and ignores the way everyone ignores her.

Ghosts pay attention to her. They're happy to talk to her because everyone ignores *them*, too.

She missed presenting her career project while she was away, but she doesn't mind so much. People think she's weird enough now anyway without her insisting that ghosts are real. Everyone just says their parents say they don't exist, and Shelly is tired of trying to convince people that their parents don't know everything.

So it's surprising to see Grandma talking with Isabel's mother in the hallway after school.

"Shelly, would you mind if we stopped at Mrs. Lee's house on the way home?" Grandma asks. "She thinks she has a ghost problem."

Shelly looks up at Mrs. Lee then looks around for Isabel. "You believe in ghosts?"

"I believe in a lot of things," Mrs. Lee says. "I believe I don't know what's wrong with our house. My friend Anna says you helped her, and Isabel says Shelly's talked about you in school. We can reschedule if today doesn't work. It's an older house and— Oh, Isabel! Your friend Shelly and her grandma might be coming over for a little bit."

Shelly doesn't think she and Isabel are friends, exactly. She turns and looks at Isabel. "Your mom thinks there's a ghost problem in your house."

"Dad says it's not ghosts." Isabel doesn't quite meet Shelly's eyes. "He says it's just because the house is old."

"And the electrician and plumber said everything looks fine, but the lights still flicker and the water is always cold," says her mother. "Does today work?"

Shelly looks up at Grandma and smiles. "I don't mind."

"Today works," Grandma says. "We'd be happy to take a look and give you our professional opinion."

Even if Shelly's annoyed with her, it feels good to be included by Grandma in a *we*—to be given some respect instead of treated like she's fragile or like she's a baby.

Still, going to one of her classmates' homes to get rid of a ghost is *weird*.

Mrs. Lee offers them a ride and they get into her SUV, Shelly in the back with Isabel and Grandma up front with Isabel's mom.

"It's too bad you couldn't do your presentation," Isabel says. "It's way more interesting than a teacher or a soccer player."

Shelly shrugs. "People would've been weird about ghosts."

"My grandma died," Isabel says. "A couple years ago. It was really—it was sad, but I have a blanket she knit me, so I can remember her still. Do you have . . . did your mom give you anything?"

Shelly doesn't want to think about *remembering* her mother. That would mean her mother isn't coming back, and Shelly refuses to think that. "I don't want to talk about it."

"Sorry," says Isabel, looking down at her lap. "I *didn't* mean to make you sad."

"It's okay. You didn't make me sad." Shelly pushes down the ache in her chest that disagrees with what she said. Maybe the ghost in Isabel's house is her grandma.

Mrs. Lee drives them to the older part of town, where the

houses are all taller and skinnier with fancy windows and carved wooden borders along the roofs, and pulls up in front of a cheery red house. The paint job is new, but the house itself looks old.

"We've been living here for a few months," she says. "The real estate agent didn't say anything about it being haunted, but he didn't say it *wasn't* haunted either."

"We'll take a look," Grandma promises. "If you've got a ghost problem, we'll handle it."

Mrs. Lee leads them to the door, Isabel and Shelly trailing behind the adults.

"My dad thinks my mom's superstitious," Isabel says, glancing at Shelly. "He said if she *really* needed to hire someone to take a look at the house to feel better, she could. I told her about what you said about you and your grandma hunting ghosts. One of her friends told us your grandma helped with her house, too."

"Oh," says Shelly, stuffing her hands in her pockets. "I didn't think you believed me."

Isabel shrugs and looks down at her feet. "I don't know. If ghosts are real I think it could be cool. I think *seeing* them would be very cool."

Shelly smiles to herself. *Weird*, she's used to—cool is new.

She feels the ghost as soon as she steps into the house. It's *definitely* not Isabel's grandma. There's nothing nice feeling about this ghost at all. It's like static electricity all along her skin—a prickling sensation that makes the hair on her arms stand up and has her shivering. She looks up at Grandma, who's undoing her hair already.

"You have a ghost all right," Grandma says. "It feels like an old one."

Shelly's pretty sure Joseph and the little boy in the hotel are the oldest ghosts she's seen—the ghosts who've been around the longest. This ghost feels very different.

"I *knew* it," Mrs. Lee says, triumphant. "I knew it wasn't just because the house is old."

"Mom, calm down," says Isabel, and Mrs. Lee laughs.

Shelly steps away from Isabel and walks over to her grandma's side. "What should I do?" she asks. "Want me to try and find the ghost, too?"

"I think it's found us," Grandma says, and she's right—the ghost appears at the far end of the hallway a moment later. It *looks* like static, too, all flickering black and white and gray, not at all as settled and person-like as Joseph. It doesn't walk, just flashes on and off, on and off, getting closer to where Shelly and Grandma are standing.

Mrs. Lee steps away from them, grabbing Isabel's shoulders and pulling her back, too. She's not laughing anymore. "What's happening?"

"What?" says the ghost, voice crackling. "Who?"

"It's the ghost," Grandma says. "Don't worry. We'll handle it."

Mrs. Lee doesn't look very reassured.

Shelly reaches up to undo her hair and Grandma stops her. "I'll handle it, Shelly," she says. "You don't have to worry about this one."

Except Shelly *wants* to worry. Shelly wants to have something to do and Grandma isn't letting her. It's not fair. "I can handle it. I know what I'm doing."

"I know you can," Grandma says, "but I've got it."

"Who?" says the ghost, voice louder now, echoing down the hall, loud enough to make Shelly flinch. "Why?"

"You need to move on," Grandma says. "You've been here too long."

The ghost's attention focuses sharply on Grandma. It flashes into place in front of her, a towering column of static.

"Who?"

Grandma doesn't move. She stares down the ghost and twirls a strand of hair around her finger, reeling it in. She looks magnificent—*powerful*. Shelly wishes Grandma would give her the chance to show her she can be that way, too. "If you can't remember, you can't be here anymore."

The ghost writhes, tugging at the ends of Grandma's hair, but she's got it hooked. It flashes angrily, but it grows smaller and smaller as Grandma pulls it closer until it's more shadow than person, an echo of a ghost that once was.

"I don't know why you got stuck," Grandma says. "But you need to move on now. If you don't have a purpose, you shouldn't linger."

Lots of people think ghosts come back because they have unfinished business. Sometimes the dead are just confused about what happened, so they don't move on. Sometimes they're angry or upset. Sometimes, like Estelle, they do want to stay so they can do one last thing. But ghosts can get stuck, and that's when haunting happens.

The lights stop flickering.

"Did you get it?" Mrs. Lee asks, after a beat, when the lights remain steadily on. She sounds shaky.

Grandma turns to her and smiles like she didn't just face down a screaming ghost. "Have you got something we can feed the spirit? We'll give it a nice, warm drink to settle it down and it should move on. It's trying to leave, but it's stuck halfway between here and there and it just needs a little help."

"I could make coffee," Mrs. Lee says. "Would that work?"

"Coffee should work," says Grandma.

"Mom, can I make it?" Isabel asks. She looks at Grandma and Shelly. "We have a machine you put coffee pods into and then a drink comes out. It's really cool."

"You can make the coffee," Mrs. Lee says, and Isabel claps her hands and runs ahead to wherever the kitchen is.

The ghost is still there, leashed by Grandma and ignored by everyone in the room but Shelly, while Grandma and Mrs. Lee talk payment. Shelly can feel the weird static buzz of it singing in her veins. It hovers in place, caught in an in-between state with people who don't see it properly, who don't believe in it. She thinks maybe the static feels *sad*. The ghost tried so hard to be noticed and as soon as it was, someone decided to get rid of it. Even now it's not getting attention. It got caught and that's it—everyone is done with it.

Shelly wishes she could save the ghost from Grandma and

take it home. Maybe she could help it find the answers it's looking for. It doesn't remember who it is—maybe Shelly could help with that. Maybe she could fix things.

"Grandma," she says, interrupting the conversation she's having with Mrs. Lee. "Shouldn't we help it remember?"

"It's very old, Shelly," Grandma says. "I think the best thing we can do for it is help it move on."

"It might have unfinished business," Shelly protests. "Maybe that's why it's still here."

Grandma shakes her head. "If it did, it's had a long time to finish it before now," she says. "It's making life difficult for Isabel's family. Our job is to help it move on. It'll be better off where it's going." Grandma turns back to Mrs. Lee like she thinks the conversation is over.

Shelly frowns, squeezing her hands into fists at her sides. She doesn't know how Grandma can claim the ghost will be better off when she doesn't know what's waiting on the other side. Grandma is acting like this ghost is the same as a raccoon or a mouse—a pest, not a person.

"The ghost is *sad*," she says. "We should do something."

"We are doing something. We're sending it on to where it's supposed to be." Grandma reaches out to touch Shelly's arm and Shelly takes a step back, away from her, as Isabel returns with a cup of coffee.

"I'm going to wait outside," Shelly says. "You don't need my help."

"Shelly—" Grandma reaches for her again, but Shelly ducks away, heading down the hall and out the door. She doesn't think the ghost should have to leave and she doesn't want to watch it go.

Grandma doesn't follow her out.

• • •

The sadness Shelly felt looking at the static ghost stays with her. Mrs. Lee drives her and Grandma home, but Isabel doesn't come for the ride so Shelly's alone in the back seat.

When they get home, Shelly tells Grandma she's going to do her homework. She can't stay in the kitchen and pretend she's not sad about Isabel's ghost. She pauses outside her mom's room, wanting more than anything to curl up on the bed with the photo she took from the flowery frame. It's still tucked away in her backpack. But if she goes into her mom's room now, Grandma will *know* the ghost upset her. Grandma doesn't need any more reasons to keep Shelly away from ghost hunting.

Shelly pulls herself away and heads to her room to play with the ghost cat and dog.

Estelle looks up at her when she walks in and says, "You're home late, kid. Does your grandma know?"

"I was *with* her," Shelly says, and leaves the room to work in the kitchen instead. She doesn't feel like listening to her complain tonight. It's easier to sit in silence with Grandma.

Grandma makes hot dogs for dinner because it's quick and easy. She looks tired.

"Shelly," Grandma says, setting the ketchup on the table. "I need to talk to you."

Shelly swallows, hoping Estelle hasn't given her ghost collecting away, and looks up at Grandma. "About what?"

Grandma takes a seat at the table. "I've been doing the budget," she says. "We're okay right now, but we might have to move to a smaller place if I can't pick up a little more money from jobs. I didn't want it to be a surprise for you if that happens."

It's not Grandma finding her ghosts, but it's not *good* news either.

"I don't want to leave," Shelly says. What if her mom comes back and they're gone? What if she ends up being a fuzzy, static ghost like the one in Isabel's house, confused and sad and not sure what's going on?

"I don't want to leave either, but we might have to," Grandma says. "We're okay for now, but just in case—"

"We shouldn't have to leave our house because Mom died."

Shock flashes across Grandma's face, like she wasn't expecting Shelly to be so blunt, but it's *true*. They shouldn't have to leave.

"It's only a maybe," Grandma says. "It's not for sure. You don't have to worry about it now. We don't have to talk about it anymore tonight."

She picks up the ketchup and squeezes it onto her hot dog. "Okay," she says. "Thanks for the warning. I'll try to be prepared."

Grandma's announcement fills her with a new sense of urgency. She can't wait for her mother to appear anymore. Shelly needs to find her before they leave and her mom becomes lost and anchorless, searching for a family that's left her behind.

16

Grandma has a job on the weekend. She walks Shelly next door, and Shelly waits 15 minutes then tells Mrs. Potts she's not feeling well and she's going to go home and lie down. Mrs. Potts is more trusting than Grandma is—maybe it's having a police officer for a daughter. Shelly leaves her house and heads straight for the bus stop. She needs to see Joseph and she's not going to wait around for her grandma to suggest a trip.

Besides, if she goes to the graveyard with Grandma, she's not going to be able to ask the questions she wants to ask, and Joseph might bring up Estelle.

The bus drops her off by the cemetery, and Shelly ties her hair up in a bun as she heads toward Joseph's grave. She doesn't see any other ghosts wandering around yet, but maybe she's just not looking hard enough. Maybe her mother's here, somewhere, and hiding.

"Little Shell, you're here alone again." Joseph pushes a

button on his Walkman and music clicks on. A singer Shelly doesn't know sings something she doesn't recognize—*alone again, naturally.*

"Joseph, have you seen my mom?" Shelly asks. "She hasn't come home, and I don't know—how long do you think it'll take for her to show up?"

Joseph tilts his head, his dark eyes boring into her. "No hello?"

"Hi," says Shelly, sitting on the grass in front of him. "Sorry, just—Grandma says we might have to move and we *can't* move before I find her. How will she know where to find us if we do?" Grandma didn't say anything about moving out of town, but Shelly's pretty sure it's what she meant. "I don't want to leave her behind."

"I'm sorry, but I haven't seen her," Joseph says, after a beat. "There's been no new souls walking. Not since the last time you were here. Did Estelle leave?"

Shelly thinks about Estelle in her bedroom. She's only got a cat and a dog and sometimes Shelly for company, but that's a lot more than Joseph has. He's been out here, alone, for a long time, with just his music.

She doesn't want that for her mother.

"Estelle's sticking around for a while," she says. "She's staying in my room." Shelly pauses. She could get in trouble if Joseph tells on her. "We're friends, right? You won't tell Grandma?"

"Are we friends?" Joseph asks. "Little Shell, you didn't even say hello. You didn't bring me a tape. You don't want me to be your friend. You want me to watch the graveyard for you. You want me to be your employee, like Old Lady does."

Shelly frowns. There's some truth to what Joseph's saying—she wants information from him—but he's wrong. "I'm not employing you. I just—I want to talk to you. I want to talk to someone who understands and Estelle just complains about how bored she is."

"Yeah," says Joseph. "She did that a lot here, too. Don't you have friends? Alive friends? Friends who know about death from where you're sitting? You're spending too much time straddling two worlds, Little Shell. You're spending too much time all wrapped up in death."

Shelly's starting to get annoyed. "This is important, Joseph," she says. "I need to find her. Who cares how much time I spend with ghosts? This is what we *do*."

"Is it?" he asks. "Where's Old Lady?"

"Working." Shelly scowls and pushes herself to her feet. "She's working because she's *always* working now. She's so busy with ghosts and making money clearing houses that she's got no time for me."

"Maybe you should be talking to Old Lady and not me," Joseph says, reaching up to run a hand through his curly hair. "I can't help you with your grandma, Little Shell."

"I don't *want* help with her. I want help with my mom!"

But Joseph's not going to help. He's being stubborn. He sits on his grave and looks up at Shelly, a little sad and a little weary in the face of her outburst, and Shelly can't take it anymore. He doesn't understand. He doesn't understand being frustrated and trapped the way she is, even though he *should* because he's stuck sitting on his grave day after day.

She turns on her heel and leaves—walking across graves in a straight line to the gates and out to the bus stop. If she wants to talk to someone who understands her, she needs to look elsewhere, and there is only one ghost Shelly can think of.

• • •

Shelly rides the bus into the heart of downtown. It's getting late, but the sidewalks are still busy with shoppers and people heading home from work. They pay Shelly no attention as she walks among them, her pace slow and steady, and hunts for the dead.

There are all sorts of ghosts in the world. Old and young, all different races and genders and everything else. Some so faint they're just smudges and some almost as solid as living people, ghosts you can only tell are dead because they have an uncanny quality that sets them apart—like Joseph and his eyes. There are all sorts of ghosts, but in the downtown core, where the living congregate in droves, Shelly can't even feel a whisper of one.

The living are overwhelming. They take up space, they're loud, and they don't notice Shelly. They ignore her in a way the dead don't because the dead are Shelly's friends, no matter what Joseph says.

The hotel's green copper roof stands out in a sea of glass buildings. Shelly uses the roof to navigate her way to the hotel and pushes her way into the lobby through a rotating glass door. When she's working with Grandma, adults don't pay Shelly much attention; they're too focused on Grandma.

And when Shelly's alone, adults assume she's on her way to meet her parents. It's a kind of invisibility that makes it easy for her to slip past the concierge and head for the elevator.

Shelly remembers which elevator the boy rode in. She remembers the look of resigned frustration on the bellhop's face when the boy ran his hand over the call buttons and slowed down the car. The living are always concerned about time, about running late and running out of it. Ghosts are hardly ever in a rush to get anywhere.

When the car arrives and she steps inside, the boy isn't there, but Shelly's worked with enough ghosts to know how to encourage him to come out. She hits a button for the top floor and lets her hair out of its bun, winding a strand around her finger.

The boy appears as the elevator passes between floors 5 and 6. The first thing he does is press every button between 7 and 30.

Shelly can't help grinning. Estelle would like him. He haunts the hotel the way a ghost in the movies would.

"Hi," she says. "Do you want to talk? I bet you're bored." It's a long shot and she feels silly doing it, but Shelly reaches into her pocket for the photograph of her and her mother. She holds it out in front of her. "Have you seen my mom?"

The boy turns to look at her, frowning. He's a solid ghost, well established in the hotel. Shelly has read the story in the book the hotel manager gave them—it says that the haunting is perpetuated by a young woman who jumped from the building's top floor. She was beautiful, according to the story, which increased the tragedy. Even sadder, she'd had a young son.

The boy doesn't look like he wants to help her. "Who are you?"

"My name's Shelly. Please, I want to find her."

"I haven't seen any moms," the boy says as they roll to a stop at floor 11 and the doors open then close again. "I haven't seen anyone interesting in forever. Why aren't there any toys? Why won't anyone play with me?"

"I'll play with you," Shelly says. "Will you look at my photo?"

"I don't want to play with *you*," the boy says, but he looks at Shelly's photo anyway. The boy shakes his head, flickering in and out of focus, like the ghost in Isabel's house. Shelly feels a spike of alarm shoot through her. He's upset. "I've never seen her before. Have you seen my mom? Where did she go? She left me here, didn't she? She left me *all on my own!*"

Shelly takes a step away from the ghost, pressing her back against the elevator wall. The lights flash off and on. "My mom left me, too. That's why I'm here," she tells him, raising her voice. "I'm looking for her!" He seems like he's in his own world. She gets the feeling it doesn't matter what she says because the boy isn't really listening.

"Who *are* you?" the boy asks. "Why are you here? Why won't you leave me alone?"

The car shakes. All the unpressed call buttons light up as the light fixture in the ceiling above them goes dark. Shelly's never been stuck in an enclosed space with an angry ghost before. She doesn't often *see* angry ghosts. Usually they're nice to her. Usually they want to move on or they want to talk, happy to be finally noticed by someone.

Shelly thought she and the boy would be able to talk. They both lost their mothers. They're both waiting for something to happen. This is different from how things are supposed to go. This is different from how she's supposed to interact with ghosts. "Where am I?" the boy asks. "Where's my mom? Where did she go?"

"I don't know!" Shelly says. "I don't know what happens next! I don't know where people go!" Shelly's hands are shaking. She's not like Grandma. She's not going to make the ghost leave just because she can, but part of her wants to push him toward what comes next, to make him move on. He's been waiting for years. His mother isn't coming back for him.

"What happened?" the boy demands, stomping his foot. "*Tell* me!"

The lights flash one more time and then the elevator goes *ding* as it reaches the next floor. When the doors slide open, the ghost is gone. Shelly gets out and takes the stairs down to the lobby.

• • •

It's late when she gets home and the lights are on in the living room. Shelly doesn't have to unlock the door because Grandma opens it before Shelly can even get the key out of her pocket.

"Shelly," she says, her voice stern and full of anger and worry, "where have you *been*?"

"I went for a walk." It's not the whole truth, but Shelly and Grandma had secrets from her mom, and Shelly and Mom had secrets from Grandma. This is Shelly's secret.

She doesn't want to talk about the boy in the hotel. She doesn't want to think about him losing his sense of self and becoming an angry shade. She doesn't want to think she might have caused it by talking to him.

He was upset, but he'll probably calm down, at least for a little while. Shelly knows now why Grandma wanted to get him out of the hotel. If he stays angry, maybe he'll become like the ghost at Isabel's house—all anger, lashing out, unable to do anything but rage at the people who come into the space he considers his.

"I've been home for half an hour. It's dark out and Mrs. Potts said you came home because you weren't feeling well. I was worried about you." Grandma reaches out to touch Shelly's loose hair. "Your hair is down."

Shelly ducks out from under Grandma's hand and steps into the house, shrugging off her coat. "I didn't bring any ghosts home with me," she says. "Not even a moth."

"That's not the point," Grandma says. "Shelly, I don't want you wandering around alone, especially after dark. It's dangerous and you could get hurt."

Shelly takes a hair tie from her pocket and pulls her hair back into a ponytail, so Grandma will stop looking at her all concerned, the way her mom used to look at them both when they got back from hunting ghosts *together*. Grandma isn't her mother. "I just needed some fresh air."

"Shelly, promise me you're not going to go out alone again."

Shelly looks at Grandma and thinks about how they're not supposed to charge for ghosts and how Shelly's supposed to be Grandma's apprentice. How ghosts are supposed to be something they do together, but Grandma keeps leaving her behind. "Okay," she lies. "I won't."

17

Shelly stops combing her hair, and in the slivers of time Grandma lets her be on her own, she looks for her mom. When she can't find her, she seeks out the dead, and she collects more ghosts.

She walks around town and looks for the dead in dark corners and forgotten places. She snatches ghosts from alleyways and buildings and takes them home to hide in her room. She rescues them.

Shelly finds Diya outside the drugstore where her mother used to work when she goes there looking for her mom's ghost. She's a young woman with long, dark eyelashes framing snowy white eyes, the opposite of Joseph's black ones. She's distracted by something Shelly can't see, only half-present in the world, but Shelly twines a snipped-off strand of hair around Diya's wrist to stop her from wandering off.

"This place is getting packed," Estelle says, when Shelly brings Diya home.

Diya floats from Shelly's hair and immediately gravitates to the cat. "What a cute . . . This is nice," she says. "How thoughtful of you to . . . I'll enjoy this."

"Oh great," says Estelle. "She mumbles."

Diya is nice, but she's not fully grounded in the world, even with the strand of hair wrapped around her wrist. Not the perfect companion for Estelle. Not the person Shelly was hoping to find.

Shelly wanders the route her mother drove to work every morning—all residential streets to avoid traffic lights—and finds Gavin behind an old apartment building. He's middle-aged and wearing an old-fashioned suit. He's hovering beside the garbage looking forlorn. When Shelly catches his attention, he looks confused by the state of the world around him. "I went for a walk," he says. "I could swear I was just in the park."

"There's no park around here," Shelly says. "Why don't you come with me? I've got someplace better for you to stay. Someplace not by a dumpster."

Gavin tilts his head, looking at Shelly like he doesn't understand what she's asking of him, but he nods anyway and lets himself be caught up in her hair.

• • •

"Another one?" says Estelle, when Shelly snips Gavin out of her hair later that day. "This is getting ridiculous."

"Oh, hello," says Diya, to Gavin. "I don't suppose . . . I'm just not sure where . . . Hello."

"I was in a park," Gavin says. "I was in a park and then suddenly I wasn't. I don't understand. Where are we now?"

"Another excellent conversationalist, I see," says Estelle. "Where's that book of crossword puzzles, kid? I need something to do with my time and they're not exactly riveting company."

"They needed someplace to be," Shelly says. They don't deserve to fade away and be forgotten. They deserve to be noticed. Shelly can provide that. "This can be their home now."

"This is *my* home, too," Estelle says. "Do I really have to share it with them?"

"You like the cat now," Shelly points out. "You'll get used to them, too."

Gavin loses track of where he is and who he's met and who he hasn't all the time. Diya can't seem to hold on to a thought until the end of it, but they're nice and they do their best to reply when Shelly talks to them. They're nice in a way that Estelle *isn't*, even if neither of them is as aware of their surroundings as she is.

Estelle complains about the company Shelly's making her keep and the lack of things to do. She complains even when Shelly buys a book of crossword puzzles and leaves it out for her. "I can't lift a pencil," Estelle says. "How do poltergeists do it? Teach me more about that, kid. I want to haunt something properly."

"You're a *ghost*," Shelly says, annoyed. Estelle is never satisfied. If Shelly teaches her about poltergeists, things will just get worse. "Anywhere you are is properly haunted."

"You know what I mean," Estelle says. "I want to see what I can *do*."

Shelly isn't afraid of ghosts, but she's never had one haunting her bedroom before. Estelle needs a distraction, so Shelly does the one thing she can think to do—she goes ghost hunting again.

She doesn't go downtown or to Zhou's or to her mom's work. This time she goes to the thrift shop. Sometimes when people throw out old things, ghosts go with them on their way to find a new home—confused spirits Shelly and Grandma used to snip off objects and bundle up to set free later.

Shelly finds Terry tucked away in a rack of warm coats. He's an old man who wears a fleece vest and squints at Shelly like he can't quite make her out. The air around him crackles with static electricity and he keeps reaching up to play with his hearing aid.

"Young lady," he says, when he notices her looking at him. "I don't believe I know how I got here. Where am I? You know, I thought being dead would be more exciting. The movies make it look fun."

Shelly knows he's perfect right away. "My friend Estelle thinks being dead is boring, too," she says. "Do you want to come meet her?"

Terry tilts his head and looks around the store. "Why not? It's got to be more interesting than this."

Shelly takes Terry home with her. When she opens the door, she freezes in place, her heart hammering. Grandma is right there, wrist deep in a chicken. She glances over her shoulder at Shelly then returns her full attention to making dinner. "Welcome home," she says. "We're having chicken for dinner."

Shelly takes a breath. "Okay," she says, trying to sound normal as she edges toward the hallway and her room. "I like chicken."

"We can make sandwiches with the leftovers," Grandma adds. "I might invite Edna over."

Shelly doesn't want to get stuck in a conversation. Any second, Grandma could stop stuffing the chicken long enough to notice Terry. "Okay," she says again, shuffling sideways to hide Terry behind her back. "I'm going to work on my homework!"

When she reaches the hall, Shelly turns and speed-walks to her room, so she can let Terry out of her hair.

"Oh, hello," says Diya. "It's been . . . Hello."

"Do I know you?" asks Gavin. "I'm not sure where I am."

Estelle rolls her eyes. "Not another one."

Terry looks down at Shelly. "Which one is Estelle, the rude one or the vague one?"

Estelle looks shocked. Shelly grins. "Estelle, this is Terry," she says. "I thought maybe the two of you could talk. He thinks death is boring, too."

"It is," Estelle says, her voice firm. "There's nothing to do and hardly anyone can hear you speak."

"Tell me about it," says Terry. "I've been stuck in a store for two weeks."

"I was in a graveyard." Estelle smiles at Terry. "Let me tell you about my angel."

Shelly's room is crowded with all her ghosts and sometimes it's hard to sleep, but Grandma is always working or tired from working. Shelly likes having the company, even if more and more it seems like the ghosts are concerned with each other and not with her. Even if sometimes, in the middle of Estelle and Terry chatting and Gavin and Diya interrupting with their half-formed thoughts, Shelly still feels lonely.

The weight of all the ghosts she's carried back to the house in her hair is enough to make her head ache every time she thinks about them. She hides them in the dresser in her closet when she leaves for school and leaves Estelle free to keep an eye on them—Estelle knows to hide from her grandma, even if she's nasty sometimes, and she's bossy enough to tell the other ghosts what to do.

Still, she'd rather spend time with her ghosts than with Grandma, who speaks too carefully to her now, or at school, where everyone except Isabel acts like they've forgotten how to talk to her at all.

• • •

"Do you think you could teach me to see ghosts?" Isabel asks Shelly before class one day. "Maybe during recess? I have an extra pack of Gushers."

"It's a family thing. I can't teach you," Shelly says. She's never known anyone outside of their family who can communicate with ghosts the way they do. It's something that gets passed down, a skill and a tradition. "And you don't get rid of *all* ghosts."

"Why not?" Isabel asks. "They're dead. Don't they have to move on? You could tell me more about them, right?"

"I don't really feel like it," Shelly says. "I like to read during recess."

Isabel leaves her alone after that.

Isabel knows about ghosts, but she doesn't *understand* them like Shelly does. And she keeps trying to talk about her parents and how her dad still doesn't believe in ghosts, but her mom's convinced. Shelly doesn't really want to talk about family right now.

Shelly doesn't really talk to anyone. She ignores the other kids at school, and everyone but Isabel returns the favor.

When she's not at school, Shelly wanders the streets. She finds ghosts and she brings them home—another cat and two dogs, a squirrel that skitters out of a bush and chirps at her feet, the faded memories of ghosts that were once people and are now just impressions of emotions: fear, longing, acceptance, confusion.

"This is too many ghosts for me," Estelle says, when Shelly brings the raccoon home. She has to elbow Diya out of the way to get to Shelly. "You're hoarding now."

"I'm not," says Shelly. "I'm making sure you aren't forgotten."

Shelly ignores Estelle's complaints. She builds up her collection spirit by spirit. She finds ghosts, but none of them are the one she's looking for, and more and more the collection feels too heavy to carry.

Grandma keeps leaving her with Mrs. Potts and Mrs. Potts won't let Shelly out of the house on her own anymore, although she *does* let Shelly come with her on errands. They go to the grocery store and Mrs. Potts gets Shelly a chocolate bar. They go to the thrift store and when Shelly drifts to the back corner and spots a tape by a band called Siouxsie and the Banshees, Mrs. Potts buys it for her, amused.

"It's very appropriate," Mrs. Potts says. "I didn't know you had a cassette player at home."

Shelly just smiles and slips the tape into her pocket.

• • •

Maybe Shelly was unfair to Joseph. Of all the ghosts she's talked to, he's the most sympathetic, and he's the only one who still acts like he sees her. Maybe he *doesn't* know what it's like, losing someone from this side of death, but Shelly wasn't very polite to him before and it's nice to be able to talk to someone who acts more or less normal around her.

She waits until she's sure Grandma's asleep, like the night she got Estelle, and then slips out of bed and pulls on clothes.

"Are you going to bring back *more* ghosts?" Estelle asks, poking her head out of Shelly's closet. "Really?"

"I'm not bringing anyone back," Shelly says, checking to see that she's still got the tape. She's annoyed at Estelle for assuming that's what she's doing and for sounding so judgmental about it. "I could if I wanted to, though."

She leaves her room and the house, locking the door behind her, and sets out into the cold night. Shelly can see her breath in the air as she walks down the street as fast as she can, heading toward the cemetery. It's no less scary the second time around, but when she gets to the graveyard she relaxes. When she's surrounded by the dead, she's safe, even if the moon is the only light she has to guide her. She has more in common with them than she does with most of the living.

Shelly picks her way over to Joseph's grave. He's not there, but she digs the tape out of her pocket and sets it down. "I'm sorry," she says. "I was rude."

Joseph is there, suddenly, closer than she expected, like maybe he was waiting for someone to visit.

"You were," he says, taking the tape from the ground and examining it. He pops open his Walkman and slides the cassette inside. A song starts playing from his headphones as soon as he snaps it shut, a mournful woman singing about a happy house. "Good choice, Little Shell. Apology accepted." He looks up at her. "Should you be out at this hour?"

"I'm not a baby," Shelly says. "I wanted to see you. I wanted to say sorry."

Joseph hums along to the song, his voice mingling with the singer's. "I *do* like this apology," he says. "I like this song. You ever heard Siouxsie and the Banshees before?"

Shelly shakes her head. "It just looked like your kind of tape. It reminded me of—you know, the one you gave me."

"The Cure," says Joseph. "Similar hair. Sit, Little Shell. Listen to some music."

Shelly sits because it would be impolite not to and because she's not looking forward to her walk home. She huddles up in her coat and listens to the sad, twanging music coming from Joseph's headphones. It's a lot like the tape he gave her. Not the same, but something about the guitar and singing reminds Shelly of the sad dance-party song her mother sung along to that last time in the car.

"My mom liked your tape," she says, when the first song finishes. "She liked music, too. She was always trying to find good stuff in the thrift store and then Grandma would steal her tapes and bring them to you."

"I think I would have liked her. Your mom," Joseph says. "I like you and Old Lady. Sounds like she'd be cool, too. Especially if she knew her music. Bet we would've been friends."

Shelly hasn't gotten to listen to music much since her mom died and this is . . . nice. It's cold and being out at night is scary, but this isn't so bad. Talking about her mom with Joseph doesn't hurt as much as Shelly would have guessed.

She smiles at Joseph. "Mom said you seemed committed to your theme," she says. "She didn't like ghosts much, though."

Joseph laughs. "I guess I am committed. Except the music came before the ghost thing. I didn't *mean* for this to happen. Was she not like you and Old Lady?"

"She was like us." Shelly thinks back to her mom, complaining about ghost lessons and Grandma. She looks down at her hands. "I think ghosts made her sad."

"We're dead," Joseph says. "Makes sense. I mean, talk about commitment—we lived our lives and now we're just here, waiting, hanging out even though nobody ever notices or talks to us. It is sad, don't you think?"

Shelly thinks about the way she's treated by people at school—by everyone. Her heart clenches. "Yeah," she says. "It's a little sad. I'm here, though. I notice you."

Joseph smiles. The translucent skin around his black eyes crinkles up. "And I appreciate your company, Little Shell."

The tape is 40 minutes long. Shelly knows because she stays and listens to the whole thing before she heads back home in the dark.

18

Shelly does her best to hide the ghosts from Grandma. She keeps burying them in her dresser when she's not home. She tucks them into her hair and her clothing when she walks into the house, so she can carry them down the hall without being stopped. Her room slowly fills up.

Most nights Grandma makes dinner and they eat together while Grandma tries to talk to Shelly.

"How are you?" she asks.

Shelly shrugs and pokes her pasta with a fork. "Fine," she says.

Grandma lets her get away with it.

"I have a job tomorrow," she says, instead of pushing Shelly for more details about her day. "I thought you might like to come with me."

Shelly looks up, surprised. "Really?" she asks. "What kind of job? Is it interesting?"

Grandma smiles. "A family keeps finding things knocked

over in their apartment. They say they have a poltergeist, so it's probably a bird."

Sometimes, birds crash into the windows of tall buildings and their spirits pass through the glass without their bodies. Birds can be destructive because they flap around trying to get free and throw things about.

It's not interesting work at all. Another animal. Shelly wants to tell Grandma that she's gotten good at people, that she has a room full of them to prove she can do bigger things.

"Birds are boring," she says, instead. "They just squawk until you catch them and put them outside. They give me a headache."

"Birds are a good way to make a living," Grandma says. "Birds will always crash into buildings."

"I guess I'll come." Shelly looks down at her pasta again. It's boring work, but at least she'll get to go again. "Do you think there are a lot of chicken ghosts on farms?"

• • •

The bird family is nice—it's two women with a little girl. They offer Grandma and Shelly lemonade when they arrive and walk them to the living room of their high-rise apartment.

"I thought it was just Maria throwing her toys around at first," one of the women says, as she shows them the cracked glass in picture frames that were knocked off the wall. "Hannah or I would put them away on the shelf and then they'd be scattered everywhere when we got in."

Hannah nods. "When we found the pictures all knocked off the wall, we knew Maria wasn't just trying to get out of trouble. She's only four. She can't reach them."

"Besides," says Hannah's wife, "two days ago we were watching TV and something knocked it over."

The bird is sitting on the top of a bookshelf. Its feathers are ruffled up and it looks about as disgruntled as a bird can look. Grandma hands Shelly her lemonade and takes down her hair.

"Don't you worry," she says. "We'll see to your poltergeist problem."

Birds aren't like people. They're harder to catch because they fly around and you can't talk to them and convince them it's time to move on. Then you need to find someplace to release them. Grandma creeps toward the bookshelf, clucking her tongue at the bird like it's a shy cat. It hops back, away from her, wary, and Grandma stills and coos at it again.

Shelly wonders what they look like to the women who hired them—and to all the other clients who've seen her and Grandma hopping around chasing phantoms. Weird, probably, but they get stuff done. She and Grandma always earn their weirdness.

Shelly puts the lemonade down on the coffee table and picks up a throw pillow from the couch. She moves around the edges of the room, past Hannah and her wife, who look worried. She waits until she's sure the bird is entirely focused on Grandma, and then she whacks it with the pillow off the shelf and into Grandma's waiting grasp.

Grandma bundles her hair up around the bird and holds it there until she's sure it's caught. She straightens up and smiles at Shelly. "Good job."

Hannah, in the doorway, looks a little confused. "Was that you catching it?" she asks. "You're done? I thought there'd be more to ghost hunting."

"We caught it," Grandma says. "We'll take it with us when we go."

"If it's really gone after this, it's two hundred dollars well spent," says Hannah's wife. "I'll get my wallet."

• • •

Shelly kind of wants to keep the bird. None of the ghosts she has hidden in her room are birds.

"We'll let it out at the park," Grandma says. The bird is still disgruntled but too wound up in her hair to escape. "It can fly around without hurting anything until it gets tired and decides to move on."

"We could take it home and feed it," Shelly says. "We have lots of milk."

"It's just a bird, Shelly," Grandma says. "If it wasn't for people sticking tall buildings overywhere, it wouldn't be here at all. When I was a girl you never saw as many bird ghosts around as you do now. Everything was lower to the ground then. It wasn't nearly as confusing for them."

"Just because it's a bird it doesn't matter?"

"Because it's a bird we should take it to a park with lots of trees and other birds and let it go free," Grandma says. "Ghosts like it aren't meant to stay forever. Most of the time it's better to let ghosts fade. You know that."

"Sometimes ghosts deserve to do their haunting. Some things need haunting."

"True," Grandma agrees. She's the one who taught Shelly that. "But those ghosts will let you know. You know that, too. Those ghosts know where they are. They know what they're about. You know the dead, Shelly. Most ghosts don't realize what's happened to them. They just need a hand getting to where they're going."

Shelly thinks most ghosts are pretty stupid.

They walk to the park and Shelly watches Grandma let the bird out of her hair. She watches the bird take off, straight up into the sky, and keeps watching until she loses sight of it in the clouds. Grandma keeps her eyes on Shelly.

19

Shelly's still thinking about the bird at school the next day. Thinking about things *other* than class is a lot easier than paying attention, especially when she knows the other kids are whispering about her behind her back. It's easier to ignore them. Then she can pretend she doesn't care. The living change all the time. They switch sides and opinions, get older, taller, decide to dye their hair, or move to new houses. The dead are better. They stay the same.

If Shelly were a ghost, she'd want to be a poltergeist. She'd want to throw her weight around and spook everyone who didn't think ghosts were real. She'd want to have *fun* with it. She can picture the confused look on Lucas's face if a ghost threw an eraser at him.

She gets where Estelle's coming from.

The bell goes for recess and Shelly pushes her chair back. Recess is just more daydreaming time for her now. It's sitting on the steps and pretending to read a terrible parapsychology book while she eats her snack. She'd almost rather sit through class with no breaks at all.

Before Shelly can stand, Isabel grabs her arm. Shelly nearly jumps.

"Hey," Isabel says. "Do you want . . . I know you like to read during recess, but my mom made cookies. Do you want one?"

Shelly gives Isabel and her hand a surprised look. "Cookies?"

"Yeah," says Isabel. "They're oatmeal chocolate chip. She used to put walnuts in them, but I told her some people at school are allergic to nuts and she can't put them in my lunch if she's going to put nuts in them and she doesn't anymore so . . ." She shrugs. "They're better now. They're good. Do you want to try?"

Shelly likes nuts, but Isabel is being nice. Isabel is the only one at school who'll talk to Shelly the way she used to. And today there's no ghost talk, no dead mom talk, just a cookie.

It reminds her of visiting with Joseph, only Isabel's playing Shelly's part, bringing her an offering to try to make friends.

Shelly keeps her opinions on walnuts to herself and smiles at Isabel, feeling a little lighter for the first time in a long time. "That sounds good. Maybe we could play a game, too. If you want."

Isabel smiles back. "I'd love to."

• • •

When Shelly gets home from school, Grandma is waiting for her, covered in ghosts. Shelly's whole body goes cold, like someone dumped a bucket of ice water over her head. Grandma looks angry.

Shelly's mind races. She doesn't know how Grandma found the ghosts. Maybe Estelle got tired of sharing Shelly's room with other spirits. Maybe Grandma was putting laundry away. Maybe she finally let herself feel the way death was piling up in her house and followed it to the source.

It doesn't really matter how she found them. What matters is that Shelly's good mood is about to be ruined. Grandma says, "Shelly, we need to talk."

Grandma's voice is stern. She's holding herself stiffly, like it's taking a lot of energy to keep so many ghosts in one place.

Shelly thinks about denying the ghosts for a moment, but there's no point lying now—Grandma has them. She went into Shelly's room and dug them out of her dresser and filled the kitchen with them. Looking at Grandma through the hazy veil of ghosts surrounding both of them, it's hard for Shelly to believe she fit so many into her tiny room.

She can't tell if Grandma has let some of the ghosts go already or not. She sees Estelle and Diya—and Gavin and the cat—but the kitchen is packed to the brim with spirits.

The kitchen is so full it makes Shelly feel like she's drowning from the weight of the dead. It's a heavy feeling in her chest that reminds her of why she started collecting in the first place. She was helping them, *protecting* them. She was gathering up company that noticed her when nobody else would—Grandma included.

"Those are *mine!*" she snaps. "You had no right going through my things!"

"I told you that you had too many of us," Estelle says, from behind Grandma's shoulder. "You should have listened."

"They aren't yours," Grandma says. Her hair is writhing with ghosts. "They belong to themselves and they *don't* belong here."

"I invited them here and they want to stay," Shelly says. "I can't tell them anything about where they're going next so why would I make them go? They're happy here!"

Diya and her wide white eyes look bewildered. "Oh, this is . . . I didn't mean . . . I think I'd like to go."

Shelly thinks Estelle was right, not liking Diya.

"You've got to let the dead move on when it's their time. The living and the dead both need that." Grandma reaches for Shelly's shoulder and Shelly flinches. Grandma pauses then drops her hand. "I know I told you that you needed to know how to care for the dead, but you've got to take care of yourself, too. You can't surround yourself with the dead all the time. You're still alive, Shelly."

Shelly scowls. Grandma is the one who breaks her own rules now. She's a hypocrite. "*You're* always with the dead."

"No, Shelly," Grandma says, her voice all soft and full of pity "I'm always with *you*."

All of Shelly's anger rises to the surface. "That's not true!" she says. "You leave me behind when you go on jobs. You're so busy worrying about money and rent you didn't even notice me hiding ghosts. You didn't go looking for them, and you didn't—" Her chest heaves. "You didn't go looking for Mom. You just *left her*."

Nothing is the same as the way it was before her mom died and Shelly hates it. She just wants her mom to come back and be her mother again. The dead don't change, but the living do, and Shelly's sick of it.

She turns on her heel and runs out of the house.

• • •

Shelly goes to the cemetery. She has her bus pass and doesn't know where else *to* go. Her ghosts are gone and her mother is dead and she's maybe not coming back after all. The cemetery is the only place she might find the answers that nobody else will give her.

She spends the bus ride with her hands clenched in her lap and her face hot with anger, thinking about Grandma clearing out her room. Her ponytail feels like a live wire on top of her head, buzzing with possibility and hanging too close to her neck.

When she reaches the cemetery, she storms up to Joseph's grave. He's sitting and murmuring to himself in French as a soothing female voice plays from his headphones. "Where is she?" Shelly demands. "Where's my mom?"

Joseph looks up with his black eyes and frowns. "Your mom's not here, Little Shell. I promised I'd tell you if she were."

"No," Shelly says. "This is where she's buried. This is where she'd be."

"Just because you're dead doesn't mean you're a ghost," Joseph says. "Look at all these graves, and still—just me."

"Why?" Shelly demands. "Why you and not her? If a bird can be a ghost, why not her? Where did she *go*? Where does *anyone* go?"

Joseph looks terribly, terribly sad for a dead teenager who talks through a Walkman. "I don't know," he says. "This place is all I know. I've always been here."

"You were alive before," Shelly says. "You're not even that old. You have a tape player."

"This is all I remember," Joseph says. "This place, which is mine, and watching over the graves for Old Lady and now you. Did you bring me any more tapes?"

Shelly's hands curl into fists at her sides. "Why would I bring you a tape when you're no *good* to me?"

Joseph tilts his head. "*Je me souviens*," he says. "I thought we were friends now. Why do I have to be useful?"

"If we're friends, you shouldn't need a bribe to answer my questions." Shelly's voice is shaking. Her whole body is shaking. Everything is coming apart around her, and all she wants is her mom. "If we're really friends, tell me what I need to do to find my mom. Tell me what you did that she didn't do! Tell me why she didn't want to stay for me! Tell me why some people become ghosts and some people leave. Tell me why you're still *here*, Joseph!"

"*J'ai peur!*" The sound from Joseph's headphones changes abruptly to music that sounds rough, angry, jagged, and frightened. Shelly steps back, unsteady on her feet. "I'm *scared*, Little Shell. That's why I'm here. I don't know what's out there. I don't know what's on the other side. I've been here forever and nobody can tell me what's there for sure. I told Old Lady, I told her I was working my way up to it. That I'd leave when I'm ready, but right now I'm *not*.

"I don't know why some people stay and some people go. I don't know why I stayed, except I was less scared of being a ghost forever and being stuck here, alone, than of whatever comes next." Joseph's music isn't even music now—it's just harsh, clashing noise. Shelly didn't mean to upset him this much, but she doesn't feel bad about it either. She wants answers.

"Maybe your mom figured it all out. Maybe she wasn't scared of death and she decided she'd had enough. Maybe she didn't want to be a ghost—or she didn't get a choice. Maybe you should spend less time worrying about ghosts!"

This isn't what Shelly came to hear. Joseph was supposed to have answers. Joseph sits in a graveyard all day, watching people come and go. He's been around for *years*. If there's anyone who should know all the things Grandma doesn't, it's him.

Instead, Joseph is just a scared, uncertain ghost like all the other scared, uncertain ghosts she's met. He feels as stuck and invisible as she does and it's *not fair*.

Shelly lashes out and kicks her foot through Joseph's immaterial body and he topples over from the force of it, coming uprooted from his spot on the ground by his grave. Joseph looks startled—at moving, at being suddenly unmoored, suddenly ghostly in a way he wasn't before. He flickers, like the man who Grandma once dredged up from the river.

"Little Shell, what did you do to me?" Joseph asks, mournful as he twists in place and tries to claw his way back toward his grave, his spot. "Where have you put me?"

Panic claws at Shelly's throat. She didn't mean to—this *isn't* what she planned. For all she's been taking ghosts and bringing them home with her, she's never taken someone who didn't want to come—she hasn't broken a rule like this before.

She doesn't know how to fix it.

"I'm *sorry*," she says. "I'm sorry, Joseph."

Shelly does the only thing she can think to do and catches Joseph up in her hair. She turns and runs from the cemetery. She runs home, back to Grandma, who will know what to do.

20

When Shelly gets home, Grandma is sweeping the last of the ghosts out of the kitchen. Her hair is pulled up into a tight bun and she's wearing an apron over her jeans and sweat-shirt. Grandma clearing out her ghosts doesn't seem so bad now. Not when panic is thrumming inside Shelly's chest like a hummingbird trapped in a cage.

"Grandma," Shelly says. "I didn't do it on purpose, I just got so *mad*."

Grandma takes one look at Shelly's frightened face and Joseph in her hair and puts her broom down. She looks sad, tired. "There's nothing to do, Joseph," she says, voice gentle. "We'll give you some milk and help you get to where you're going."

Shelly carries Joseph into the kitchen and sits with him at the table, trembling and quiet and sorry, while Grandma pours his milk. Grandma sticks the mug in the microwave and turns to look at them, rubbing a hand over her face. "How did this happen?"

"I didn't mean to," Shelly says quickly. "It was a mistake."

"I made her mad," says Joseph. "I told her I was scared."

Shelly's panic has calmed, but now all she feels is crushing guilt. Joseph wasn't supposed to be uprooted. He was supposed to be allowed to stay until *he* decided to leave. Even if she and Grandma have both been breaking other rules, this one is going too far. Joseph isn't an angry shade or confused wisp of a thing. He's not floorboards full of mice or a raccoon in the chimney. He's a person with thoughts and feelings and he's scared—like Shelly's scared—of the big unknown waiting for him.

Grandma sets the mug of warm milk in front of him. "There's nothing wrong with being afraid," she says. "But you've been in the graveyard for a long time."

"Yeah. Maybe this is a sign it's time for me to go." Joseph prods the mug with a finger. "I'd rather have music. I don't need feeding."

"You could stay here," Shelly says, even though she knows Grandma won't approve. "I can keep you here. You should only have to leave when you're ready."

Joseph looks up at Shelly. There's no music coming from his headphones now, just his voice, and something about that is more distressing than if he'd been playing a sad song. "No," he says. "No, I don't think I can stay. We're supposed to be friends, right? I don't think staying is what a friend would do, Little Shell."

"We carry our dead with us everywhere we go," Grandma says, reaching out to touch Shelly's hair. "The important people don't leave us, even when their ghosts are gone. Even if they never come back."

"Do I get to be important?" Joseph looks at Shelly, lips smiling nervously. "You'll remember me, won't you? I gave you a good tape. Introduced you to new music. Sat with you in a graveyard at midnight. That's worth getting remembered."

Shelly's hands are shaking. She can feel her heart pounding in her chest and she wants to say no. She wants to tell Joseph he needs to stay around if he wants her to remember him. She wants to tell Grandma that memories aren't the same as a person. That they fade. One day she won't remember the sound of Joseph's voice through his headphones. One day she won't remember her mother's face. Maybe ghosts aren't the same as living people, but they're better than *nothing*. She wants to wrap herself up in them and hold them close. She wants to keep everybody here, with her, instead of letting them leave.

"I don't want you to go," she says. She's trying not to cry, but when she blinks a hot tear rolls down her cheek. "*You* don't want to go."

"I know," says Joseph. "But I think I have to."

"We'll remember you," Grandma promises. She takes a comb from her apron pocket. "Are you ready?"

"I don't know," says Joseph. "But I guess most people don't get to decide, do they?" He cups the mug in his insubstantial hands, looking down at the milk inside it. "I'm as ready as I'll ever be."

Joseph is right. Death is something that happens to everyone, but knowing when it's going to happen, choosing when you make the transition from life to death, choosing whether or not you'll be a ghost and stick around a little longer, isn't something most people get the chance to do. Shelly's mom didn't get to decide when she died. And unless she comes back, Shelly isn't going to get the chance to say goodbye to her the way she's getting the chance to say goodbye to Joseph now.

It's not much, but it's a small comfort.

"I'm sorry." Shelly reaches out to touch the mug in the same spot as Joseph's cold hand. "I hope wherever you're going is nice. I hope you like it."

Joseph looks at Shelly and smiles. "Yeah," he says. "Me, too."

Grandma combs Shelly's hair and Joseph gets blurrier and blurrier until he fades away. Just before he goes, he tilts his head to the side, looking startled. "Oh," he says, his voice like static. "I hear music."

And then he's gone. Shelly blinks hot tears off her eyelashes and Grandma keeps combing her hair until her tears stop falling.

"Do you feel better?" Grandma asks, handing Shelly Joseph's milk, now just lukewarm.

"No." The kitchen feels empty without Joseph. The *house* feels empty knowing she doesn't have a crowd of ghosts waiting in her bedroom, but without their cold weight it feels warmer, too. The ache she's been feeling from filling her hair and room with ghosts isn't there anymore. Something has changed. Shelly's not sure if that's good or bad.

21

Shelly and Grandma sleep in Mom's room that night—or Grandma does, anyway. Shelly lies awake with her back to Grandma, staring at the shuttered blinds over the window and thinking about Joseph. Joseph said that staying with her wasn't what a friend would do. Maybe he was right, but it's still not fair. It's not fair that Shelly's mom died. It's not fair that she hasn't come back. It's not fair that Shelly didn't even get to say goodbye to her, like she did to Joseph.

If Shelly could have one last conversation with her mom, she'd tell her she should be a ghost. She'd tell her she should stick around and be here with Shelly. That this is where she belongs.

Shelly would say she misses her. She'd say she loves her.

Her mom would say she didn't mean to leave so soon. She'd say she loves Shelly, too. And Shelly knows she'd say she wishes she could stay, but the dead aren't meant to stick around.

Shelly rolls over so she's facing Grandma, squeezing her eyes shut as she starts to cry. When she makes herself really think it through, it's obvious—Mom isn't coming back. Her ghost isn't going to show up one day. Shelly's been chasing her mother's ghost, looking for her everywhere, even some places that didn't make sense. But she's moved on to whatever comes next and Shelly's been chasing after something she's never going to find.

Shelly's mom didn't like ghosts very much. In the photo Shelly has in her backpack, the one of her and her mom when Shelly was small, her mom even has short hair—hair way too short to catch the dead. Maybe Joseph and her mom have two things in common—their taste in music and thinking that haunting Shelly would be bad for her.

Shelly inhales shakily and wipes at her eyes. Her hair feels heavy, even without the ghosts. It feels like too much to carry. Like a burden.

Except her mom had it short before, in the photo. Shelly doesn't *have* to have it long. If she cuts it, she won't be able to catch the dead until it grows out. She won't be able to help Grandma on jobs for a while. But suddenly, the thought of not having to deal with ghosts for a while just sounds . . . like a relief.

No more bringing the dead home. No more searching for her mom.

It's a way to say goodbye.

• • •

In the morning, Grandma makes bacon and eggs for breakfast. Shelly thought she'd be in trouble if Grandma ever found her ghosts, but Grandma's being kind about it. She serves Shelly and then sits down with her own food, watching Shelly pick at her plate.

"I know you're upset about Joseph and the other ghosts," Grandma says, "but they had to move on, Shelly."

"I know." Shelly looks up at Grandma. She's upset, but she understands better now. Mostly she's thinking about the decision she made the night before. This morning, she's certain. "I want to cut my hair."

Grandma pauses with her fork halfway to her mouth. "Your hair?" she repeats. "Shelly, are you sure? That's a big decision."

Shelly *is* sure. Even just saying the words feels right. It's time to cut her hair so it can grow out new and shiny, not tangled up with the dead, not dragging at her shoulders with the weight of the memories it carries. "Yes," she says. "I need to."

Grandma hesitates, then nods. "Okay. Do you want to wait? So you're really sure?"

"I'm really sure," says Shelly, because she is. She wants it gone. "Can we do it now? Please?"

Grandma sets her fork down. Her expression is a strange mix of pride and sadness as she looks at Shelly across the table. "Okay. Get the scissors from my sewing kit and we'll get started."

Shelly grabs Grandma's little silver scissors and they go outside to sit on the front step. It's late enough in the year and early enough in the day that it's still kind of dark out. The sky is pink-purple-red as the sun comes up. It's pretty, and Shelly watches the sunrise while Grandma combs her long hair out one last time.

Grandma gathers Shelly's hair into little ponytails and cuts them off carefully, her touch gentle, and hands Shelly each lock of hair as she goes, until they're all gone.

Shelly shivers when the evening wind brushes her neck, and shakes out her newly shorn hair, feeling the crisp ends brush against her skin. All the things she's been carrying with her are still there, but they seem lighter now. Easier.

Shelly winds the strands of her hair around and around her hand. There's so much that isn't attached to her the same way anymore, and now she can't fish for ghosts as she walks the street. She can't load her shoulders with the weight of their lives. She can't kidnap anybody from a graveyard. As much as she might want to, she can't chase her mother's ghost. She has to admit to herself now that her mom wouldn't want her to.

"I'm sorry I yelled at you," she says, looking up at Grandma.

"You have your mother's temper," Grandma replies, smiling at her. "She'd be proud of you for telling me exactly how you were feeling. It's okay, Shelly. I'm sorry I didn't see what you were doing. I promise to listen better in the future."

Grandma touches Shelly's hair, brushing her fingers through it. "I used to cut your mother's hair for her too, when she was little," she says. "She never wanted to catch ghosts. She always said if she spent all her time hunting them, she'd never have time to do anything else. When she had you, she cut it short again. She said taking care of you was more important than taking care of the dead. She said she let it grow out again because keeping it short was too much trouble. I think she liked the idea of being able to help you if you needed her to." Grandma's voice is sad, but her hands are steady.

"Shelly, whether or not you catch ghosts, you're still my granddaughter. You're still your mother's daughter. Part of the gift our family has is knowing when you can take care of ghosts and knowing when you can't. I'm proud of you. Your mother would be proud of you, too." Grandma leans down and presses a kiss to the top of Shelly's head. "We took a lot off. What do you think?"

Shelly's hair is gone, but all the feelings from before are still there. They just hurt a little less. She hasn't seen what it looks like yet, but she knows the answer to Grandma's question already.

She smiles up at her. "I like it."

EPILOGUE

The day of the first snow of the season, Grandma and Shelly go to the thrift store and to Zhou's. They buy a tape—The Smiths' *The Queen Is Dead*—and get an order of sweet and sour pork with a side of fries to go. Then they get on the bus and head to the cemetery. They're moving to a smaller apartment soon, but for now it's the same route and the same number of stops as it was the first time Grandma brought Shelly here, when she met Joseph.

Shelly's okay with moving. Her mom never liked the orange wallpaper anyway. Things her mom *did* like—like the posters she put up in Shelly's room—are coming with them to their new apartment.

Shelly's gloves are so thick she can barely bend her fingers, and she's all wrapped up in her winter coat, but the air outside is cold enough that having the bag of takeout on her lap is nice—kind of like having a hot water bottle made of fried food and foil containers. She's still getting used to the way her new, shorter hair leaves her neck exposed to the wind.

"It'll have to be a quick visit," Grandma says, as the bus pulls up outside the graveyard. "It's too cold to stay out here long. I don't want you getting sick."

Shelly smiles at Grandma and helps her off the bus. "That's okay," she says. "I just want to say hello."

The cemetery is deserted—no ghosts or other people lingering—and Shelly and Grandma follow the winding paths to Joseph's grave first.

It's small and flat. It looks empty without Joseph there. Shelly dusts snow off the little metal plaque that marks his final resting place and sets the tape Grandma hands her down beside it.

"Grandma thinks you'd like this one," she says. "She says my mom liked them, and you had the same taste in music. I bet it's better than French tapes." She reaches for Grandma's hand. "I hope wherever you are now, you like it. I hope it's nice after you waited so long to go."

There are a lot of things Shelly wishes she could say to Joseph's face. There are a lot of things she wishes she could say to her mother, too. There's so much she wants to say, wants to know, and now every new thing she's going to learn about her mom will be from moments like Grandma picking up a cassette and telling Shelly her mom liked The Smiths. She's glad Grandma shared that, but Shelly still wishes she could have learned it *from* her mom. Maybe she understands, now, why her mom chose not to come back, but that doesn't make it easier to accept that she's gone. Even more unfair than not getting to say goodbye to her mom is that Shelly doesn't get to share her life with her.

Ghosts are echoes of the person they once were. They fade away, slowly, personalities and memories eroding over time. And they're invisible to most people. They can't talk or touch unless something happened to make them exceptionally motivated to try.

Her mom wasn't afraid of what came after death—she was afraid of being stalled, of being stuck in between the place she came from and where she was going. Her mom was afraid of being an echo of her living self.

Shelly gets that. She hoarded away people she didn't even know—Shelly pulled Joseph from his grave and brought him home with her because she didn't want to let go of things and she didn't want to change. Shelly wanted to be a static, unchanging thing. She wasn't a ghost, but Shelly let herself become a haunted place, gathering ghosts around herself like a safety net, like maybe they'd let her get closer to her mom, but that was the wrong choice.

Her mother made her promise, that day they'd listened to The Cure in the car, not to get too caught up in the dead. She made Shelly promise that she'd have fun and be a kid, too.

Shelly's got time to get better at that now. It'll be a while before her hair grows back.

Grandma squeezes Shelly's hand and they continue down the path to the newer part of the cemetery, where Shelly's mother is buried. There's a plaque here too, shiny and new, and Shelly lets go of Grandma's hand so she can wipe the snow away from it.

"Hi, Mom." Shelly opens up the bag of takeout, prying open the containers. It smells sweet and savory and delicious—it reminds her of her mother even more strongly than the smell of her shampoo or the sheets and duvet in her mother's room. It reminds Shelly of the good memories she had with her—the secrets they had together that are no longer just Shelly's to keep.

She sets a couple pieces of pork and a few french fries on

her mother's grave. "I brought your favorites. I asked, but they don't do milkshakes to go. Grandma says on my birthday I can invite Isabel and we'll go and eat in. I'll order an extra milkshake for you then." She pushes herself to her feet. "I love you," she says, and Grandma rests a hand on her shoulder, squeezing gently. The ends of Shelly's short hair brush against her neck in the wind, making her shiver, and she leans against her grandma for shelter from the cold. "I miss you, but I'm okay."

ACKNOWLEDGMENTS

There are some stories you carry with you throughout your life. For me, hearing my mom and grandfather talk about the police coming to my great-grandmother, Louisa, for help finding missing people in Chapleau was one of them. Louisa's story stuck with me and transformed first into a short story and now into a novel. First and foremost, I want to acknowledge her for the role she played as inspiration for Shelly and her family, and my grandfather, Gordon Byce, for passing her stories down to me.

This book wouldn't be possible without my parents, who let kid-me read anything I wanted as long as I was reading, and who supported my decision to get two degrees in creative writing. Thank you for letting me buy terrible Most Haunted Places books even though I couldn't sleep after reading them, and to my brother, Cory, for also liking spooky things. I know I made Shelly an only child, but I promise it was nothing personal.

Thank you to my publisher Annick Press for their support, and especially to my editor, Claire Caldwell, who had faith that a short story could become a book, and without whom *The Ghost Collector* wouldn't exist. I'm grateful to Claire for her insight and guidance, and for reaching out to me to begin with.

Writing a book is a marathon of a process and often boring if you're not the writer, so a special thank you to my friends Grace Lee and Sarah King, who listened patiently while I obsessed about pacing, and to Ben Rawluk for being my writing buddy for the last eight years and for talking through countless plot problems with me. An extra-special thank you to Isabel Kim, who read my drafts and told me they were good, except where they weren't, and who accidentally loaned Isabel her name and love of coffee machines.

Allison Mills grew up in the suburbs of Vancouver, where she spent a lot of time reading novels under her desk at school and bickering with her younger brother. As the daughter of a teacher-librarian, Allison had easy access to books of all kinds and developed a deep appreciation for writers like E. Nesbit, Diana Wynne Jones, and Ursula K. Le Guin. She also spent a lot of time scaring herself with spooky stories, a habit that grew into a lifelong fascination with ghosts. She sympathizes with them. As someone who's both Ililiw/Cree and settler Canadian, Allison knows what it's like to straddle boundary spaces. This preoccupation with all things ghost-related inspired her first novel, *The Ghost Collector*.

Despite all her covert in-class reading, Allison did like school quite a bit and now has three master's degrees, including an MFA in creative writing. She aims to create stories like the ones she loved to read as a kid, but with more kids like her in them. When she's not writing, Allison works as an academic librarian and archivist.